THE NEXT SECOND COMING

THE NEXT SECOND COMING

A NOVEL ABOUT JESUS' RETURN

MARK HATTAS

The Coalition
POWERED BY THOUGHT LEADERS PRESS

ISBN: 979-8-9929366-9-8 First Edition, 2026 Printed in the United States of America (hardcover)

ISBN: 979-8-9929366-7-4 First Edition, 2026 Printed in the United States of America (paperback)

ISBN: 979-8-9929366-8-1 (e-book)

For more information about the author, visit theocoalition.com

For permissions inquiries: mark@theocoalition.com

WHAT READERS ARE DISCOVERING

AWARD WINNING SERIES

The O Coalition Series is a sweeping spiritual fiction saga: Christ-centered modern parables that unfold as encounters—where the reader doesn't just follow the story, but awakens within them.

The series guides readers to Jesus' teachings in practical application, leading characters (and readers) through brokenness to restoration — revealing pathways to spiritual alignment, healing, and gifts while God becomes intimately, undeniably real.

PRAISE FOR THE O COALITION BOOKS

BOOK FOUR

"The Jesus in these pages isn't the one I grew up with at a podium. He's the one I always hoped was real — the friend who shows up, says the true thing plainly, and leaves you stronger for it. ***I'd put this in the hands of anyone, churched or not."***

— JAMES CHITWOOD, D.M. OWNER, PERFORMANCECULTURE.EXPERT

"This is storytelling with a calling. In an age hungry for meaning, Mark Hattas writes fantasy that feeds the spirit.

His worlds are imagined, but the truth running through them is as real as anything you will ever encounter."

— ERIC HIMES, FOUNDER AND PRESIDENT, THE INSPIRED CULTURE

*"I **couldn't stop reading**. It's **compelling and daring**, and pulls every thread of the book together beautifully — a deep and profound offering, **one of its kind**. I grew up with a lot of ambivalence around religious communities, and even so, this perspective gives me hope and reassurance that I have a place where I fully belong. **It moves me, inspires me, and makes sense to me.**"*

— GENE HUNEYCUTT, RECOVERY COACH + STORYWORK PRACTITIONER

*"This book met me where I was — and didn't leave me there. It mapped a path to authentic trust, leading well beyond fear. God has always been calling. After this book, **I felt a true surrender — a level of trust I didn't have before.**"*

— GINA JOHNSON, CEO/FOUNDER, GJ TRADING COMPANY

*"The Next Second Coming is an extraordinary and engaging novel with an intriguing plot. The **story unfolds with quick, unexpected turns that kept me reading with real anticipation.** I found myself wondering whether humanity would rise to the moment or collapse into destruction. The **journey and its conclusion genuinely surprised me.**"*

— JOSEPH GABRIEL, CHIEF OF STAFF AND AUTHOR

*"**Each book in The O Coalition series has gone deeper than the last**, and this one goes the deepest. You don't need the others, but if you have read them, the emotional payoff is real."*

— MELISSA G. WILSON, FOUNDER AND PRESIDENT NETWORLDING PUBLISHING

*"**Great read!** In a world dominated and blinded by fear and darkness, Mark **Hattas shines a bright light on the divine process of love that can transform** a disconnected, broken humanity into a powerfully connected one being made up of every race, tribe, and nation."*

— BRAD LIVELY, FOUNDER, TRUSTLOVE COACHING

*"A supernatural gift! **Hattas really hits the mark with this one.** Not just once, but again and again throughout. He provides an invitation — not only a good story but initiation into right relationship with Divine Love (God, Jesus). Transformation is inevitable!"*

— ANGIE BRUCE, MA, HARMONIZING WHOLENESS

"A great way to reflect on how God continues to move on the earth and in our lives for the betterment of all."

— KEITH A. LITTLE, HONORARY PROFESSOR AT PCUA (PONTIFICAL CATHOLIC UNIVERSITY OF AMERICA)

"However you think of the second coming, Hattas' story will help you ***keep your way, while expanding understanding*** *to a whole new level."*

— JIM MCGOUGH, EDGEONE MEDICAL & EDGEONE VENTURE PARTNERS

BOOK THREE

"Mark Hattas has crafted something rare: a novel that operates as both compelling narrative & practical spiritual roadmap. Through Thomas's journey as a wartime healer, the book reveals a clear method-ology for accessing God's voice and unlocking extraordinary gifts. The wartime setting serves as powerful metaphor: the real war is internal, between who we're trained to be and who God created us to be. The tools are real—releasing control, forgiving perceptions, seeking God internally—and immediately applicable. Highly recommended for seekers ready to move beyond theory into lived experience of divine union."

— STEFAN JUNAEUS, FOUNDER, THOUGHT LEADERS PRESS

BOOK TWO

"The Veil Breaker is a surreal and emotionally raw journey through mental collapse and spiritual rebirth… I'd recommend it to seekers, to survivors of trauma, to anyone who's had a brush with mental illness or spiritual transformation and wants ***a book that gets it.*** *Not in a clinical way, but in a gut-punch, soul-lifting, what-the-hell-just-happened kind of way".*

— LITERARY TITAN ON BOOK TWO

BOOK ONE

"Heartfelt and thought-provoking… a blend of mystical experiences and relatable human struggles makes it an excellent choice ***for readers interested in spirituality, mental health, or personal growth."***

—LITERARY TITAN ON BOOK ONE

CONTENTS

ORIENTATION

The Next Second Coming is a gentle and entertaining reminder that something in you is ready—a latent transformation whose time has come.

The world can look insane. It has left many of us confused, numbed, and quietly destructive — to ourselves and to each other. And not so quietly destructive—*nation against nation.*

Yet we can do something about it. Jesus showed us a path, a practical framework for this transformation into your best self.

Imagine a caterpillar refusing its chrysalis out of fear — numbing itself, distracting itself, anything to avoid the dissolve. Is that healthy for its future? No. Nor for us. And yet that is what has happened.

This is not a time to blame. It's a time to act.

Let's change together and embrace the life God is calling us to — the life God is calling you to.

— MARK

"This is the State of Jesus"

These words came to me when I first asked, What is this? — when I encountered a relationship with Jesus beyond my understanding. I offer this book in that same spirit, from that state revealed to me.

-MARK

CHAPTER 1

GOD, ARE YOU THERE?

"Be still, and know that I am God."
— Psalm 46:10

"God, are you there?"

"Sit, my son. Quiet your mind. Be still."

The voice came the same way it always did—not from the clouds or the walls, but from somewhere deep within.

It wasn't always that way. When he was a teen, John was learning to become a machinist. His mom had passed. He was only seventeen. His anger was palpable. God tried speaking to John then, but he couldn't hear.

For months, he numbed his *grief* with carbs, alcohol, and depression. Waking with greasy fingers clutching a remote—potato chips by his side—and ten pounds added to his waistline, John needed help. His father was absent, ill-equipped to help his children mourn.

Anger, hurt and resentment hadn't been John's nature, but became an emotional cocktail at the ready for months following his mom's death. All that, plus pouring himself into work, had drowned God out.

Every week, at the machinist shop, a young man, no more than twenty-three, invited John to his church. John repeatedly said 'no'... until a *misfire.*

John was cutting through a tractor frame with an angle grinder. The blade spun at 10,000 RPM when the metal shifted, pinching the blade.

He'd seen what happens when one of them goes wrong — the disc kicks back at the person holding it. He'd seen the scars.

As the tool jumped from his hands and shot toward his face, time slowed down. The power cord caught on a tractor hitch, instantly yanking the plug from its socket. The motor died mid-air. The disc spun down and thumped hard against his leather apron.

Time returned to normal, but his heart hammered. He looked down at a scuff on his apron and imagined how horrible the situation could have been.

He sat down on the shop floor, looked up, and yelled, "I'll go. I'll go."

He went to church and gave thanks for the near miss. Within weeks he lost the weight. His friend sat with him in the shop after hours, week after week. He let John be angry. He let John be quiet. One evening, for the first time since his mother died, John cried all the way through and didn't shut it off. It was during that mourning process that he heard God for the first time.

He doubted at first, thinking it was his own mind, but the evidence mounted and his trust grew. Now, as an adult, his relationship with Christ, with God, was like that of a great teacher: accessible, real, and unhurried.

Years later, an adult now, John asked the same question to begin every prayer. "God, are you there?"

This time the answer came, "Sit, my son. Quiet your mind. Be still."

The church echoed with his footsteps as he took a seat among the circle of empty chairs. Light filtered through the windows. Evening services wouldn't begin for another hour. A car passed outside. Inside, it was still.

John sat, worn.

"Close your eyes," the Lord said. "Watch."

John breathed. He had learned to center in these moments without pressing. Only receiving. After ten minutes, the darkness behind his eyelids gave way to an inner sight. He didn't seek or understand it. A city materialized. Then a year appeared, emerging as light from the dark.

1517 A.D.

The light in Jerusalem softened in the early evening. It was amber and heavy, making the old stone appear lit from within. Jericho felt it on his face as he climbed the steps toward the

Church of the Holy Sepulcher—the holiest ground in Christendom for some.

He had come to pray, as he did many evenings. The Ottomans — the new conquering force — had hired him to design works for the city, and the weight of their expectations pressed on him daily. The most recent commission, a plan for Jerusalem's water supply, sat heavy on his mind.

Prayer was needed.

He did not expect company.

A woman appeared at the entrance. Her aura seemed to dance. It caught his attention. She was looking right at him. A stillness settled between them.

"Praise be to God." She said as he approached.

"Praise be to God." Jericho responded. He noticed she stood still, waiting for him to approach. Others passed, but she only looked at him. He stopped walking.

"Do you know…" She asked, "that Jesus was here?"

"So I'm told. I understand this is the site of His crucifixion, His burial, and resurrection." Jericho replied.

"Perhaps. Perhaps it was… though, what do we truly know?" She looked out of place—certainly not a regular. Strands of shiny black hair escaped her silk headscarf.

Suddenly, there was quiet. The streets were empty. Just the two of them.

"Who are you?" He asked. "You don't look familiar."

"He is coming," she said. Her voice was calm and certain. "In three days. Prepare a place."

Suddenly, movement returned. Jericho looked at people arriving and moving past on either side of her, entering the church. None of them paused.

"Who—" he started. But he already knew. And when he looked back, the woman was gone.

That evening when he prayed, he felt the truth in her words. For three days he prepared. He shared the good news. He found a place.

Three days later, a crowd gathered at the Damascus Gate Plaza. They sang hymns and worshiped.

The man who arrived was not what the city anticipated. There was no procession. No spectacle. A path opened. A widow lowered her shawl. A child tugged at the man's tunic. He lifted the giggling boy high above his head, drew him in for an embrace, and set him down. He ruffled the boy's hair before continuing to the front.

He was handsome, powerful. His presence carried strength beyond the physical. It was unmistakably Him. Jericho stood near the back of the crowd, the space he had prepared now full of people who had come from every corner of faith — and doubt.

He watched their faces and movements as Jesus spoke. That is what stayed with him long after the day. Not the words, but what happened to people's demeanor when they heard him. Everything twisted in them seemed to come undone. Years of tension, uncertainty, and confusion melted away.

Jesus told them he had always been with them. He welcomed every soul present, regardless of their beliefs.

In the days that followed, Jericho discovered something in himself that hadn't been there before. Or, perhaps it had always been there, unripened or buried deep within.

He forgave his brother, and on his way home invited a hungry beggar to join his family for dinner. After dinner, the beggar offered to help fix a leak in Jericho's roof. "I've been after Jericho about that leak for weeks." His wife said with a smile to the beggar.

As the week progressed, the weight from work lifted, his shoulders eased, and ideas flowed easier. He grew more present, more jovial. He saw the good in people. He became a teacher in the markets, gentle, generous, slow to judge. All this goodness had been obscured by life challenges. Jesus uncovered it.

The days leading up to Jesus' return had been dark. Many had given up. But hope returned as those who witnessed the encounter became like lamps, carrying the stories with them as they moved through their days. A new age of discipleship arrived.

John opened his eyes slowly and took a deep breath. The chairs were still empty. A clock showed only a handful of minutes had passed. His hands rested on his thighs.

"God, what are you showing me?" He asked.

"Jesus is returning." The words crashed like stones breaking the surface of still water. "You must prepare."

John's breath caught. He took a full breath, and then another. He realized his hand was shaking and pressed it flat against his thigh. *Jesus is returning* echoed in his mind.

A fire was lit in him. He sat with the words, 'Jesus is returning'. His system settled. He was re-centered, and God spoke once again, "There's more. Close your eyes."

CHAPTER 2
THE RELIC

"Now faith is the substance of things hoped for, the evidence of things not seen."
— Hebrews 11:1

John closed his eyes again. A new date appeared:

1932

Maurice hustled—panting and scared. His pursuers were catching up. The mountains of Israel had been hot and rough with its steep, rocky terrain—treacherous to navigate by foot, especially at speed. There was no place to hide.

Maurice was a famed European inspector in Jerusalem on a case. He couldn't have anticipated being the one hunted and found.

Khalid and his crew surrounded him.

"You scoundrel," He said to Maurice. Sweat dripping, Maurice finally sat on a nearby rock and caught his breath. Linen suit torn. Panama hat in one hand. A handkerchief in the other wiping his brow.

"Gentlemen. I think there's been a terrible misunderstanding. I'm not here for you. You have nothing to do with the cult I'm investigating."

The men exchanged glances. They shrugged. Expressions, faint but certain. No urgency in them. After all, they had their guy.

"You don't remember us." Khalid said. "You were here a few years ago—as a soldier. We know you. The scar on your face. My brother put it there."

He and his brother smiled at each other.

Years earlier Maurice had supported Jewish activists asserting ownership of the Western Wall. He was among the soldiers imposing curfews and restoring order in the wake of the Western Wall Riots.

"Yes… I remember." He studied their faces. Perhaps it was

the panic, but Maurice moved to compliment them. "You've... done well for yourselves." Breaking the tension didn't work. A knife thrust toward him with no mercy. He was just one of the group's targets hunted down after the riots.

The cave was no wider than a man's shoulders.

Khalid pressed his back against the limestone and held the lamp closer. The sound of Maurice's body being dragged nearby quieted as he inched inside. Old dust, and the smell of something sealed away forced a cough. His three companions waited at the entrance—there wasn't room for more.

They had come to dispose of the body. Instead, they found an opening into the mountain. Remnants on the trail below were evidence that a landslide must have revealed it. Khalid noticed the narrow gap in the rock face above the trail. He had almost kept walking. But something pulled his eye to it, the way a detail in a room pulls your eye before you understand what's wrong. He'd taken the lamp and gone in alone.

The sunlight shifted. A single ray angled through the crack above and fell across the cave floor, and in its path lay clay jars, most of them shattered. Carved stones half buried in the dust.

One jar remained sealed. Its stopper was dark with old bitumen, the clay still intact. Beside it, a rolled piece of linen, fragile to the touch. And beneath that, catching the light: a bronze medallion, illustrated, about the size of a man's palm.

Khalid picked up the jar. It was lighter than expected.

He studied the medallion next, turning it in the lamplight. He couldn't read the images clearly in the dark, but something about the symbols and figures etched into it made him set it back down carefully, rather than pocket it. It showed a gathering of people. A cross. Distinct letters. It felt sacred. He didn't know why... but he did not want to be the one to disturb it.

He brought everything out into the daylight and showed the other three before securing it in his satchel.

Unsure of its value, the men brought the relic to George, a well known antiquities dealer in Jerusalem's Old City.

George opened the jar. Inside was hair tied neatly and wrapped carefully in a delicate linen. Faded Hebrew letters could still be made out along the cloth.

George leaned over the table for closer inspection. He looked again. Then again.

"Wow!" George said.

"Wow, what?" Khalid asked. "Is it valuable?"

George went silent — eyes withdrawn, fingers tapping the workbench.

Then he said to Khalid, "Can you fetch Brother Matteo? Quickly. He'll know what this means. He'll be at the monastery on Mount Zion."

"The one who's always barefoot?" Khalid asked.

"No, the other one with the patched up robe."

Khalid returned with Brother Matteo and they all marveled at the inscription: "This ______ is of our loving Lord, God of power and might. His return gave help and hope in our hour of need."

The missing word was assumed to be hair—the holy hair of Jesus.

"This is it! For the Love of God. May I see that medallion, please?" Brother Matteo asked.

George framed it in the light on his workbench.

"It says here," Matteo said, "that Jesus visited a gathering in 1517 A.D. Miracles happened. Darkness lifted. Wounds healed. Disciples were unleashed." He smiled with great elation.

"May I have it?" He asked "To send to Rome?"

"No." George quipped back. "If this is authentic, it's bigger than you. Bigger than Rome. We must do right by it."

"Yes, yes. Of course."

"And what about payment?" Khalid asked. "It must be worth a fortune."

"I've always done right by you, Khalid. I'll do the same now." George assured him.

George quickly consulted Dr. John Garstang of the British Department of Antiquities. He and his team authenticated the relics. Their paleographic study dated them to the early sixteenth century. Right time. Right place. Convincing.

Given its sacred nature and sensitivity to local tensions, the relic was placed under safekeeping at the Palestine Archaeological Museum.

Brother Matteo wrote a private letter to Rome relaying the story, stating, "My hands tremble as I believe I have seen the most profound relic in centuries… The inscription speaks of His return in a time of tribulation, and it's hard not to read in those words a message meant for our age… My heart fills with hope that our Lord has not abandoned us during our time of strife, just as our friends were not abandoned in their time… May God grant the grace and wisdom to receive this gift with faith and prudence…"

Once proven authentic, a clandestine operation quietly purchased the relics and brought them to Rome.

All parties sworn to secrecy, they have remained hidden until today—revealed in spirit to John.

"God, again, what… I… Are you serious? 1517? 1932? Jesus is returning? Now? In 2033?" John asked as his eyes slowly opened. With tension in his body high, he took another breath to calm his system.

God then said, "Jesus is returning, John. You must prepare."

The words settled in the stillness.

The church door opened.

Footsteps approached.

CHAPTER 3
OLD HICKORY

"Blessed are those who mourn,
for they shall be comforted."
— Matthew 5:4

YEARS EARLIER—BEFORE John Smith was inspired to start a church, before he knew Christ so fully, before he trusted God's voice so thoroughly—he simply wanted a good life. Happy family. Solid work. Strong faith.

John worked with his hands. He operated a machine factory in rural Kentucky, making parts for farm equipment—parts that would prove tough to come by as wars would eat up resources later in the decade. The physical labor kept him grounded.

Janie gardened, took care of the children, and monitored her mother's health. That is until her own health declined.

Janie died suddenly in 2022 when an aggressive form of cancer ravaged her body. Once discovered, doctors claimed she had three to five years to live, but instead she passed in six months.

Her doctors hadn't seen anything like it before, and didn't know how to help. She was the first of many unusual cases in their area; all types of physical, mental and emotional diseases—aggressive like never before.

John prayed for guidance to lead her to health. He had a very special relationship with God—often receiving insights, visions or words of comfort while praying. That relationship matured further during Janie's sickness.

God told John, "She will likely pass, but you still have time. Love her every day. Bring more to your relationship now, and that will open you to more after her passing."

"What does that mean?" John asked, but no answer came. When she died she got a full-honors funeral followed by a light show of drones displaying a full color picture in the sky of her with John and their young children. The drones hummed with the LED glow of their faces at dusk.

It was all thanks to their nephew studying engineering at the University of Kentucky. His senior project involved drones and he pulled on his contacts to facilitate the gift.

After the drone show, a message remained in the sky, "Build my church."

John asked his nephew why he put that message up there, but his nephew insisted he had never programmed it—and said the drones didn't display any messages, just pictures.

The crowd murmured and thinned for the reception. John's hands shook the way they had in the hospital. He exhaled... slowly. A stillness washed over the ache, and in it he knew: the words weren't for the sky; they were for him. "If this of you, Lord," he mouthed. "Make it obvious please."

That night, John awoke to someone nudging his shoulder. He was pretty wiped out and had a few drinks. Groggy and slow to respond, he heard, "Build my church," in a soft firm voice. His eyes shot open, but no one was there.

Chalking it up to dreaming, but curious, he went about his days, adding to his daily prayers, "God, if you are calling me to build your church, then get me a building and I'll believe it. You get me a building and I promise I'll build it."

In the meantime he grieved. His children, Elizabeth (15), Carl (9), and Sarah (6), joined him for a ceremony at the bank of a local river. He brought pieces of paper, a bowl, shovel, and a small white pine tree. Elizabeth brought a blanket and snacks.

Sitting by the water he initiated an exercise that would change how he experienced grieving—very different from how his father did it. A friend told him about it and John agreed it was worth a shot. He was so broken.

Each of them wrote things they cherished about Janie on strips of paper, read them aloud and put the papers into the bowl. They followed this by writing and reading things they didn't like or still judged about Janie. This was followed by a release.

Carl read, "I hated the way you criticized me. I felt so small and unimportant... defeated. I forgive you and let go of judging you, mom." Choking up he leaned in and hugged John.

"My turn." Elizabeth said. Her sweet demeanor when celebrating how great her mother was changed to anger. "I told you to look into alternatives for treatment. I sent you articles, possible solutions, and even a doctor with success treating cancers. You didn't do one of them. And now... Ugh, I could scream!!!"

And she did. Her shrieks soon turned to tears. "Perhaps you'd be alive if you'd listened to me… and Uncle Jared. He believed. I believed. You didn't."

"Oh, Elizabeth," Sarah cried. "Why do you have to say all that?"

"It's ok, Sarah." John interjected. "Elizabeth has every right to voice her feelings. Anger is ok. It's ok to feel. Let her finish."

Sarah nodded, wiping her tears, and Elizabeth continued. "I do wish you would have listened. I'm hurting so much. We all are, and we miss you. We just want you back. I love you mom, and release my stories about what I think you should have done."

It was quiet. Just the breeze across the water. A bird fluttered nearby.

"And?" John asked.

"And what?" Elizabeth retorted

"You don't really know for certain those approaches would have helped. Mom's family has a history of cancer. We just don't know."

"I know, Daddy. I just want her back." Elizabeth broke down as she hugged her dad, melting in his embrace.

Sarah softly spoke up. "I guess… I'm mad too. Why did God take my mom?"

"Why do you think?" John asked.

"I don't know." She replied.

"I don't know either," John said honestly. "But I trust God has a plan, even if we can't see it yet."

Many tears fell that afternoon and the ceremony concluded with burning the papers and burying the ashes under the pine tree planted to symbolize Janie's everlasting life.

When they felt complete, Elizabeth drove Sarah home, and left nine-year-old Carl and John to walk together. They crossed over the river, walking slowly on the plank bridge, and up stone stairs to a forest path.

"Carl, can I ask you something?"

"Sure, dad."

"I know this may sound strange, but God keeps asking me to build a church. I don't get it. I don't know how to build a church —and not sure I want to. I like our church. Plus, I wouldn't want to do anything to compete with our church. But He keeps asking. I asked for God's help, but honestly had hoped the request would go away. Instead, it's getting stronger, pressing on my spirit."

John looked at Carl, realizing how unfair it was to pose this to his young son. Janie would have known how to help. But then, Carl asked the perfect question.

"Dad, what does God mean by 'church'?"

John sat with the question lingering. "I think I know. It's a community, a holy space, a needed place where people can practically apply the teachings of Jesus. It's not a replacement for Sunday, but complements and welcomes people from all faiths."

"Sounds nice." Carl replied. "Sounds like something God would want."

"Yeah, I suppose so. Thanks, Carl. I think the answer is to get comfortable doing God's will here, even if I fear some won't like it."

For the first time, John felt at peace when thinking about the church.

The next day at a local hardware store, Maria Domingas found John in the bolts aisle.

"Are you John Smith?" She asked.

"Yes." He replied. Maria was stunning in the purest of ways. There was something about her smile. He felt at peace right away.

"My name is Maria. I rent buildings in town and need some help. I've heard you're the best. Would you be willing to fix a radiator we're having trouble with?"

His thumb worried the thread of a half-inch bolt while Maria spoke. He found her beautiful. A wave of guilt. A pinch of fear—as if noticing another woman were the first crack in the wall he'd built around Janie.

She's just asking for help. Don't be so presumptuous. He thought. Then she said something he had only ever heard once in his life.

"Oh — and fair warning, I'm already spoken for. You couldn't pry me loose with a crowbar and two strong Baptists."

He laughed before he knew he was going to. The tension he'd been carrying since she first spoke to him left his shoulders.

"You know," he said. "There is only one person in my life who ever said that to me."

He smiled and looked back at the bolt. Maria knew enough not to pry. She waited.

A shift. A breath. He looked up.

"I'll come out and look at the radiator. It's the right thing."

They finished shopping, and he followed her truck the mile up the road to Old Hickory.

Old Hickory was a long abandoned old saloon, later restored, and now rented out for events. While there, he had a vision of the space being used for worship. Maria hadn't intended it that way, but easily pictured his vision as he explained. Despite his inner doubts, he spoke with confidence about the church God asked him to build.

"If you help me out once in a while, I'll make sure you have this space for worship once per week. How would that work for you?" She asked.

They made a deal, and John put another request on God that night. "Well, you brought me the space. I don't think I believed you would. I guess I hoped you wouldn't. God, I don't know what I'm doing. Why are you choosing me? There must be some Biblical scholar ready for this. I am just… I mean, you know me. I'm a flawed man. I don't know how to build a church. A building is one thing. What about people? I don't know how to attract anyone to a new church. Will you bring the people, Lord? Guide me here."

John didn't hear a response but his request was in *queue,* and God provided. Oh did He ever.

Because of God's provision, after John's day job in the shop, he spent his evenings as a preacher and spiritual counselor. They congregated at Old Hickory, starting out with five friends. Those friends told friends and those told more friends. Soon 50 or so people regularly attended the service on Tuesday evenings. They came from all walks of life. Most still regularly attended other churches on the weekends, but a few attended John's church exclusively. They had never found a relationship with God like at that Old Hickory Church.

By 2033 the church was thriving. WWIII had ended. A mental health pandemic compounded the war's effects, reshaping the world.

John's town had lost a dozen young men to the war. A temporary healing center from the pandemic had been dismantled. The huts and barbed wire came down. The soccer fields and baseball diamonds came back. Hearing kids at play again refreshed everyone's soul.

Schools adopted a litany of gratitude and reinstated morning prayers. Every morning the day started with, "I am thankful for my life, the food I eat, the people I love, and the God who gives me strength and courage..."

The kids seemed happier. More engaged. Less dependent on technology.

Peace, though finally stable, left a future filled with uncertainty. Things once taken for granted weren't anymore. People were still reeling, healing, helping. Despite scarcities of food, fuel, and convenience, innovations quickened. A small device could power an entire home. Grocery stores grew their produce on rooftop vertical farms — fresh daily, no trucks needed.

It was common for multiple families to live together—work together. Yards turned into gardens. People valued connection, community. And faith… faith soared.

Only a few had predicted the spiritual awakening would transform society with such ferocity.

The rapid changes weren't so obvious in John's life. His lessons were hidden. Same town. Same home. Same business. Raising children and spoiling grandchildren. Listening for God's prompts.

He'd been humbled by loss and wasn't sure he was good enough to navigate visions he believed the Lord shared with him. Nonetheless, he prayed vigilantly for guidance. He talked to God as he worked and preached.

Local farmers, decimated financially, could barely afford parts at resale let alone retail. They relied on John and his unique skillset, his steadiness, the way he could resurrect a broken implement with nothing more than a lathe, prayer, and grit.

And John still loved the shop: the smell of hot oil mixing with coolant; iron filings gathering at his boots; grit living under his fingernails. The clang of metal over the years gave his grief a rhythm. The steady heat of the machines calmed him when his mind slipped toward memories of her.

As John's kids grew up they had helped out at the church, but as they aged got busy with their own lives.

Now, Elizabeth was married with two little ones of her own. She would visit on occasion, but lost interest in the church as a priority. Carl showed up at Old Hickory whenever home on university breaks. He studied Theology at Marquette University in Milwaukee. Sarah, a junior in high school, chipped in as long as nothing interfered. Amongst cheer, school, and friends she found plenty of reasons to skip services.

After Janie's passing, John remarried Stephanie. Maria had introduced him to Steph, a friend from New York, a few years post-funeral.

Steph was the opposite of his Janie—a corporate go-getter, traveling often and more interested in deals than spiritual growth. That said, she supported him 100% and attended the weekly service when in town. Steph kept him grounded in the physical world while he stretched her into heavens.

This was Steph's first marriage and she adored John's children, never trying to replace their mom, but behaving as one would hope: Loving, nurturing, compassionate. The kids loved her as well. With mountains of airline points, Steph committed to take each of them, for their twenty-first birthday, on a world tour to her favorite spots—Spain, France, Dubai, and new to the list, Israel.

John had always wanted to visit and she arranged a sixteen-day trip for his fiftieth birthday. They needed private security for the war torn region, but they did it.

John's favorite site was on the Sea of Galilee, looking up to The Mount of Beatitudes in the Korazim Plateau. From the water he imagined how it served as a natural amphitheater for Jesus' Sermon on the Mount.

At one point, he swears he went back in time and witnessed that scene as it happened. It wasn't the first or last divine mystery in John's life.

John found that the way of spiritual mastery and the accompanying journey always led people on their most perfect path. Building a church was part of his.

From the beginning, John envisioned intimate gatherings and rich conversations—exactly what was built.

One such conversation arose at the church in October of 2033. After ten years, the church was well regarded and known in the area. The space felt grounded, holding the faint scent of lingering frankincense. The wood remained the dominant feature: sturdy and seasoned.

After the main service, it was common for people to stick around for hours. Volunteers, led by Sarah that night, reorganized the chairs into three concentric circles, allowing for intimacy and camaraderie as they prayed and discussed topics of interest.

As Halloween approached the following Monday, the evening's conversation turned to ghosts.

Sarah crossed her arms and glared at John.

He winked back with a shrug and a crooked smile.

She had texted earlier from school.

Sarah:

> ok dad i'll come tonight. practice got cancelled. but if this is a ghost story thing i'm leaving lol

John smiled and replied:

John:

Deal. Boo!

Sarah immediately sent a selfie from the school parking lot—cheer uniform half on, hair pulled back, eyes rolling dramatically toward the sky.

Sarah:

> love u dad. see u tonight

John's friend (and landlord), Maria, was a regular at the service and shared a powerful story. A few dozen listened in as she started:

"I was ten years old in our basement and the lights flickered. As I ran up the stairs, feeling nervous, I saw a party of thirty *people* or so in the basement out of the corner of my eye. I stopped and stepped back down some stairs to get a better look, but no one was there. Freaked out I ran and told my mom about seeing ghosts.

She said, "That's ok. Tell them to go away if you don't want them there. That is your basement now." I yelled that message down the stairs and added, 'In Jesus' name, get out.' I had heard a preacher say that on a street corner outside a revival tent.

My mom also called in a priest to bless the house for good measure, and our lights didn't flicker after that. I know what I saw and they were ghosts. I felt safe in the basement after the priest left. I believe in ghosts. I just don't like 'em."

"They're harmless," John's son, Carl, piped up. Home for fall break, Carl had a keen interest in the supernatural. He was under the impression ghosts were lost souls looking for connection and if we invited them to forgive themselves and ask the Holy Spirit for help, they could find a home in God. Carl had been like this since he was little—listening for things no one else seemed to hear.

Carl shared his view, and a few people shifted uneasily. John noticed the change in the room. He took a slow breath and whispered a small prayer under it. The air seemed to settle, as if the floor itself had exhaled. Then he spoke.

"The truth," John said, "is Jesus taught what is always true. He gave us a process to come into alignment with, and reconnect entirely in God. Jesus lived it, taught it, and prayed for us to experience the same union He experienced. His life is our example to be the hands and feet of Christ today."

John let that land, grabbed his Bible and continued. "The Bible doesn't describe ghosts the way our culture does — lost souls drifting through hallways, stuck between worlds. But Scripture is not silent on the dead appearing to the living.

"In 1 Samuel, the prophet Samuel appears to Saul. In Revelation, the souls of martyrs cry out from beneath the altar. And at the Transfiguration, Moses and Elijah appear alongside Jesus — so real that Peter offers to build three shelters, one for each of them, and then they are gone. What this tells me is that Moses and Elijah are alive in spirit. They are eternal, and yet we do not see them with our physical eyes unless God permits."

John looked to the ceiling; eyebrows raised and palms up, as if waiting for confirmation of his message. A nod. He continued.

"Perhaps, like an elevator, Jesus rose to the floor — the frequency — of their heavenly location. After all, his face, in that moment, shone like the sun. Perhaps that was a message to help us understand his teachings even more deeply.

"But not every unseen presence is heavenly. I believe ghosts are trapped by earthly ideas, while souls in heaven are focused on God. Carl's thought of helping these ghosts is an interesting one. I wouldn't recommend chasing after those experiences.

"That said, if you are in right-relationship with God and you are called by God to support a soul finding its way to God, then right-action is to help. But to chase for glory or honors for yourself or to 'save' a lost soul on your own is off-target. It would be like running into a burning building to save a kitten without any training or protective equipment. If your path is to become a 'firefighter', get properly trained.

"Even then, keep your eyes on God. Let us act for the glory of God, and we will find refuge in God's abundant grace and love."

John was smart, down to earth, and spoke plainly. Stories continued throughout the evening, but it was the last story that opened John to his mission outside of the church, beyond his machine shop and rural Kentucky.

It was shared by an elderly woman—her first time at Old Hickory. She had noticeably walked in with her cane ticking the wood. Her hair was silver with a red-tailed hawk feather secured by a braid. Her guest name tag read *Colette.* She attended with her daughter, Celia, while passing through Kentucky—on her route home to Nashville.

"Mom, share your story," Celia, a dark skinned woman of thirty years, urged. All eyes were on them. Celia's encouraging whispers easily overheard. "It's ok, mom. They'll love it." Celia untied a scarf from around her neck and placed it in Colette's fidgeting hands.

Sarah, bored till that point, noticed an attentive shift inside as Colette rubbed the silk scarf, inhaled deeply and looked at her daughter, "Ok, Ok. I'll share, but I don't think anyone will believe me. I don't know."

"Yes you do. You do know. Share it, mom. Share."

Colette raised her hand and nodded, affirming to herself and the group that she would indeed share. She stood and walked to the inner circle and took the speaker's seat. John adjusted a microphone to her height. Before saying a word, her presence commanded the room, as if every soul present sensed something sacred had arrived. Her frame was slight, her eyes were clear, steady, and knowing — gentle with understanding. Her skin was wrinkled and loose like the bark of an old olive tree, aged but alive with rooted strength. She spoke eloquently and with the sincerity of a top sermon. No theatrics or need to convince. Just presence. People leaned in. They *felt* her.

For a moment she said nothing. The room grew quiet, anticipating something holy about to take place.

CHAPTER 4
COLETTE

"And the Word was made flesh,
and dwelt among us."
—John 1:14

COLETTE BEGAN, "This is the true story of my encounter with Christ. I don't want you to believe me, but instead listen. If you are one who needs to hear this, you will remember it all the days of your life. If not, you will likely forget in a day or two. Many do.

"I was four years old. We lived in the hills of Tennessee. Cherubim and Seraphim filled the sanctuary during mass in my home town. I saw them every time I went to church.

They had wings—some two, some four, some six. They moved in ways I didn't understand... like energy, like light. There were wheels within wheels, turning and alive somehow, covered in eyes that saw everything. Their faces were unlike anything I had seen. Each had four faces: one like a man, another like a lion, another like an ox, and the fourth like an eagle.

She lifted up a Bible from the seat next to her.

"It wasn't until years later that I realized... it was the way Scripture describes them."

"Well that would have freaked me out." A voice whispered across the room, a bit louder than intended. A handful laughed in agreement.

"It wasn't anything scary." Colette addressed the comment. "They filled the church in a kind of ordered glory... moving, watching, worshiping. And they sang—constantly—glory to God."

Another whispered, "My God," under their breath.

Colette continued,

"Now, it may help to know I was in a Catholic church. Communion wasn't just symbolic to us. I was raised to believe, and experienced, that the bread and wine were truly Jesus... His Body, His Blood... His presence with us."

Colette chuckled at a memory. "There was a framed verse in our mudroom growing up. I must have passed it a thousand times...

'He who eats My flesh and drinks My blood has eternal life... For My flesh is true food, and My blood is true drink. (Jn 6:54-55)'

"I didn't just believe that. I saw something happening.

"When communion would begin, more angels would come. They gathered around the altar… moving purposefully like they had roles… part of something unfolding. Others stood guard around the priest… and anyone near him.

"And at the end… the roof would open. I was likely the only one who could see it, but it always opened. And there was singing… so beautiful, beyond anything I had ever heard from a choir.

"It was like that every week."

She blinked, returning, appearing surprised at the clarity of her memory. The room was quiet.

"But one week… when I was five, Jesus came out of the Eucharist… and walked to me. He knelt down and held my hand."

A man near the back leaned forward, elbows on his knees, as if afraid to miss a word.

"It was strange, and I feared Jesus was coming to take me home to heaven. My body trembled in my seat. But then He touched me and the fear departed."

"He said, 'Colette, would you like to know who you are, truly? I wish to inform you of the real you. You are more than you think. You have awareness of me that others don't have. No one else can see me in this church. No one sees the angels like you do. Do you know this?' I nodded."

Colette took a long breath.

"I knew it was true, as people gave strange looks when I told them about my experiences at church. My mom told me it would be better to keep those stories to myself, but I was five. I wanted to share."

"I know how that is!" A woman half way around the circle yelped. "My momma told me…" But she stopped, realizing her interruption didn't fit the setting.

"Well, it sounds like you can relate." Colette said. "Believing my own eyes cost me friends, yet gave me insights. I've since learned that's often the trade. I stopped telling people of the magnificent sights, even withholding from family, as my parents chalked it up to an overactive imagination."

"Mm-hmm." The same woman nodded in agreement.

Colette continued. "Despite their rejection, Jesus' message was helpful to me. It allowed me to rebuke my mind, which told me I had been making it up. With Jesus' support I told my mind the truth— just because others didn't see what I saw, it was ok. I remember accepting my unique relationship with the unseen."

John and many of the participants naturally had questions, but didn't want to interrupt her flow. She had obviously told the story before, as it had a polished feel. Fascinated, they wanted more.

"As time went on," Colette proceeded, "Jesus taught me—but only while at church. I hungered to go and spend more time with Him. He helped me grow up and understand what is true of this world. At one point He told me something shocking—that I would experience His second coming.

Colette hesitated and looked to her daughter. "Should I share this with them, honey?"

"Yes. Yes, mom. These are your people. They'll understand."

Colette nodded, sipped her water, and continued, "Ok. It wasn't until I was fourteen or so that Jesus asked me to see his message more fully. I would go to mass before school and sit for 30 minutes alone after the service, and before my classes started.

"It was a different church than I attended as a young girl, but the circumstances at the altar were identical. If you ever wondered whether a proper Eucharistic celebration changed bread to body and wine to blood, I have witnessed it thousands of times. It's real. At least, it's real for me."

"Why do you emphasize that?" A gentleman called out in the second ring of chairs. Eyes turned to him. "I mean, it sounds weird. I'm a Protestant and Communion has always been symbolic to me… and doesn't require a Priest."

Colette smiled. "Yes, I'm aware there are different views and practices for Communion. I respect yours. I emphasize mine, as it still fills me with awe. And I remember how much I missed it.

"For seven years starting at six years-old, I was unable to attend mass. I hungered so much for it—hated being apart from it. I missed the mass. I missed Jesus, but that's another story. By the time I was fourteen, I had returned to the church and couldn't get enough. It was a magical return.

"The thirty minutes following daily mass were special. I would often sit alone after mass let out. Jesus would show up and we'd talk. He'd teach me."

The same man asking about Communion raised his hand. Colette encouraged him to talk.

"Do you expect us to believe Jesus literally showed up and taught you?"

"Sam, would you just let her tell the story?" His wife scolded him.

"Well… It's just a bit beyond anything I've ever heard. It sounds fanciful." He defended.

The pressure of the rooms eyes on him increased his discomfort. "Come on people. This is pretty out there." He looked around for support.

John piped up. "Sam, I can assure you, I've seen a lot. What Colette is sharing is completely plausible, not only in the Bible, but even beyond it. Several of us in here have some unique mystical experiences. Not to mention the saints. You've heard of St. Teresa of Avila, yes?"

"No." Sam admitted.

"She was a 16th century mystic. In one of her mystical visions, Jesus offered her his hand and a nail to signify their spiritual marriage. I agree with your wife on this one. Let's hear Colette out."

"Ok. I'll listen. I admit this is all new to me."

"I thought these were my people." Colette whispered to Celia.

"It's only his second time at the church. His wife has been inviting him for years. He's new."

"Ah… ok." Colette closed her eyes and centered herself.

After a few breaths she said, "After mass Jesus taught me. Amongst the teachings, He emphasized how people misunderstood him during his life on earth. And, in the same way, He said people misunderstand the second coming. He pointed to the Bible and had me read from Matthew.

"Every day I read out loud to him. Some days we spent our entire time on one sentence as He added depth to the passages. When we got to chapter 24, though, I had a hard time. My words tangled in my mouth. He encouraged me to just let the sounds come out, even if they didn't make sense.

"It was my introduction to speaking in tongues, though at the time I had no reference for it.

"I didn't understand the sounds leaving my mouth. Later I learned that some call it the language of angels. It felt like something inside me, but beyond me spoke. The Holy Spirit, perhaps. Jesus laughed beside me. He seemed amused that all my careful attempts to pronounce the words kept falling apart.

"The sounds flowed out of me in ways I didn't understand. They weren't words I knew. Though they were rhythmic at times, an onlooker might think it was gibberish. But something holy was moving through them.

"Then the sounds gave way to English. Wisdom came out—not my normal communication style… or ability. Thoughts formed differently, like the tongues dialed a number and God was on the other line."

She chuckled. "I know that sounds silly, but it truly felt more like the words were coming through me, just as water flows from an opened faucet.

"I wrote the words down. They were too profound to trust to memory. I remember thinking and even wrote it here," Colette pointed to her notebook and read, *"Only of God could such profundity be possible.* Profundity was one of my freshman-year vocabulary words, and I was proud to finally put it to use.

"I'll read what I wrote in those days if you like; some from Jesus directly and some translations of those tongues. It took weeks to receive the messages fully, but I got them, and when I did, I understood what Jesus laid in front of me. He was coming back, but not how I had imagined."

Colette paused, glancing up to see if people were still engaged, for she had lost herself in the memory of that incredible experience. People were literally on the edge of their seats. John brought her another drink of water and she took a moment to refresh.

"Tongues, Sam? How's that landing for you?" John asked with a smile, giving Sam an opportunity to object.

"Tongues I get." He pointed to his wife and said, "Seventh generation Pentecostal sitting right here. I get the tongues thing."

John turned back to Colette. "This is incredible. I think I can speak for most all of us. We've never heard anything like your story. We definitely want to hear what you wrote, isn't that right?" He directed the question back to the group which gave a resounding affirmation.

Colette reached in her purse and withdrew an old composition notebook, the one she wrote in at fourteen.

"I picked this up in Illinois this morning where it was stored with some other belongings during the war. My best friend from high school still works at a Benedictine Monastery, and kept it safe for me."

After flipping through a few pages, she found her place. "Here it is." She looked excited. A rush of familiar emotions arose as if the first day she wrote.

Colette began: "Jesus said to me, 'I was about to be crucified and knew my disciples were missing the point of my death. That was ok, as there would be time after my resurrection to train them further with the Holy Spirit.

'I knew that gift of the Holy spirit would teach them, lead to the deeper, internal path of transformation. That, Colette is something modern society is still confused about. Most people focus on the external ways of change, muting or even ignoring the internal. The internal is where restoration resolves.

"He said, 'Resistance to this restoration process leads to external manifestations mirroring the resistance.'"

A woman near the window lowered her eyes. The words had landed somewhere painful.

"'That mirror is information that is intended to support correction. For example, if you burn your hand on the stove, you will be more careful next time. However, if you ignore the warning that fire burns, you will burn yourself again and again. Thus, you can see, resistance to this learning dishonors the truth, disrespects the flame, and puts the body in danger of repeated injuries.

"Jesus explained, 'Fire is an obvious example. The more subtle examples are in your emotions, circumstances, relationships, beliefs and more. Your outer world, Colette, will always mirror your inner world.'"

Colette lowered the notebook for a moment. No one spoke. A few shifted in their chairs.

John realized several people had stopped breathing as her words resonated something much deeper than curiosity.

She continued, "'If you believe you are separate from God, your outer world reflects separation, division. This dishonors your true nature of love, unity, wholeness. Like gravity pulls you to earth, God calls you to restoration in Him. Once there, you and God are made whole—Adam and Eve are restored in the Garden.'

"As Jesus spoke, I saw a vision of the restored man and

woman. I saw the world broken and dark come back to health and peace. The church where I sat had dissolved and given way to that vision. It was met with a sense of hope.

"Then the vision went away and Jesus looked at me and continued. 'Any subtle, or not so subtle, inner divisions, your unresolved history, must be revealed and healed. The design of the universe pulls forward the broken, unhealed parts of your life and that of your lineage and even the collective in humanity, not to reinforce your pain, but to give you an opportunity to address it. All divisions will end.'

"That one struck me," Colette said. "That all divisions will end. It gave me hope throughout my life. He went on to say, 'The right path is to release the past, heal in the spirit, forgive all sins. You may have thought I was the only one who was to do this, that I did it *for* you. I did, *and* left you a roadmap to follow me. I modeled everything and left a blueprint… a framework, but that wasn't the end. It was the beginning of the end. The end is near, Colette. It is near for all who choose this path. We are birthing an indescribable new era. I did things no human could conceive of before my resurrection. There is more to come.'

"I remember him leaning in… His eyes pristine, perfect, so peaceful. He said, 'As you grow older, Colette, you will know what all this means. But today, just write it down. Is that good with you?"

"I agreed and Jesus continued, 'As you can see, I have returned. I am here. People looking to the sky for me will wait another day, but those who prepare will find me.'"

Colette stopped reading. Carl let out a slow breath.

That last line struck a chord with John. He had heard testimonies before. But nothing like this. He felt his spirit churning as he glanced around the room. No one looked skeptical anymore —only stunned.

"'Preparation' Jesus continued, 'is key. Do you turn your oven on before baking cookies? Of course. Do you gather ingredients before turning your mixer on? Naturally. Likewise, you are to follow me and prepare. Those who do, will know me all the days of their lives. You don't need to wait for a sci-fi movie-like scene to unfold in your world to know I'm here. My return is now.

'Some, like you, will know me before the days when no one can deny me. You get to know me now. Share the good news that I have returned. Let others find me now. Let them know Christ wants to return through them. I have come. Look at me. I am who I am.' I looked at him. His sincerity was true. I melted in the eyes of God. I no longer wanted for God after that. I was with God always. Splendid! I knew my life would never be the same. Jesus continued to teach…"

"Wait a minute." John asked her to explain something for everyone. "Were you seeing Jesus physically? Were your eyes showing you a man in the church?"

"No. I saw them with an inner eye, but one day he did appear as a physical presence, just not in those early days."

"You saw *them*? More than just Jesus?" John asked.

Colette lit up. "The whole cadre of heaven was present. I was in the presence of God's holy people, angels, saints. There were a multitude of people in the heavenly church. A multitude of people."

"Amazing. Thank you," John said. "A hint of jealousy might be hitting me. My apologies. Please, continue. This is incredible."

Colette looked around before starting again. Her eyes sparkled as she returned in her soul to those fourteen-year-old experiences and read once again, "Jesus continued to teach me. He said, 'The path to oneness with God is through Christ. When I said the path was through Me, I was speaking as Jesus the Christ—not through a man separate from God, but one with God. I was the example for people to lean into, to trust.

'When people truly understand what I taught, they apply it, master it, transform, and rise up with me to union with God. Still in a body… one with God. Christ then lives in them. The person they knew themselves to be no longer exists. A renewed person comes alive in them as a Christ.

'Their self before Christ experiences death of all that is false, and embraces their new life. This is the second coming of Christ. It happens within you first. Not all will experience it identically. Some will wait for a physical return and that is their choice. However, I am here to invite those with eyes to see and ears to hear. Aliveness in Christ is available now.'

Colette knew this was a lot to share all in one sitting and paused. Scanning the room she saw recognition in some, confusion in others.

"He continued saying, 'Some are focused on the world. They don't know me and they have rejected the truth of God. This has led to efforts to mute, distort, and delay the inevitable—both individual and collective unity with God. Those people actively thwarting this are not bad. They reflect the unhealed parts of history, just like the unhealed parts in you. All will be healed.

'Those people know not what they are doing. They act as an animal would react to danger—to a loss of perceived control, to a fear of what they don't understand. There are efforts to stop people from this beautiful restoration, attempting to keep minds trapped in hell—separate from God.

'Colette, efforts to abolish my true church are real, but will fail. Every jot and tittle in the Bible is latent within you and every human being. There is nothing you don't have. It lives in the air you breathe, in the flower you enjoy, in the universe you abide in. Colette, the Lord your God lives in all things. And, if someone is unaware, you might wonder how they can become aware. Yes?'

"I agreed with Him, and what followed dismantled much of what I thought I knew."

He said, 'There is a path unlocking the secrets of humanity and I shared them. When people realize it, the Christ will actively live everywhere. God will truly bring about a new heaven and new earth. It begins in you and everyone who says

YES to Me and My Way. I am The Way Colette. And, I gave the formula for a restored life. It is a recipe and always produces the results of wholeness with God. When many people live as Christs, there will be a significant change in aggression against it.'"

"Amen!" a woman in the back involuntarily called out with her hands up in praise. Colette looked up and smiled as the spirit of God was clearly at work.

She continued with words of Jesus, "'Christ is even known in circles of darkness where forces opposed to God recognize the light of Christ. I can attest, and you'll find it in scripture, that even demons believe—and tremble (James 2:19). The leaders in these circles of darkness often sense the truth in their souls, even if not conscious of it. They chose darkness and can see light even more than some Christians because they abhor it, and a reaction happens in them, like something convulsing in the presence of light, madly dashing about to stop Christ from returning.

But the return is today and it's spreading. It will continue spreading and will not be stopped. No amount of persecution will deter it. It's ironic that the opposition fights, yet the transformation can be even more delightful in those furthest from me. This is because the contrast from one way of being to another is so significant. All can be saved, Colette. If they only knew the true God, they would never take action against another, and only with God."

Colette looked up from her notes and said, "I remember putting my pen down many times and scanning the *empty* church. My hand either hurt from writing so quickly, or it was time to get to class. I must admit I was late more than once. My teacher never seemed to mind."

"What else did Jesus say?" One of the participants called out. "Please share more."

Nearly an hour had passed, yet no one had checked their phone or glanced at the door. Instead, heads nodded in agreement for more. John asked if she was up for it.

"How long do we have?" She asked with a smile. She clearly loved sharing.

"Our group stays for the duration, Colette. We'll be here as long as you are willing. By the way, there are plenty of snacks and waters in the corner."

A few stood to stretch and refuel.

Beyond just an interesting story, John wondered if something far larger had just walked into his life. He wanted more too.

"Ok, then. Let's continue," Colette said. "We're getting to the good part now."

Several people laughed in disbelief that this remarkable gathering could get any better. Colette smiled too, knowing what was coming.

CHAPTER 5
PROPHETIC MYSTERY

"The kingdom of God is within you."
— Luke 17:21

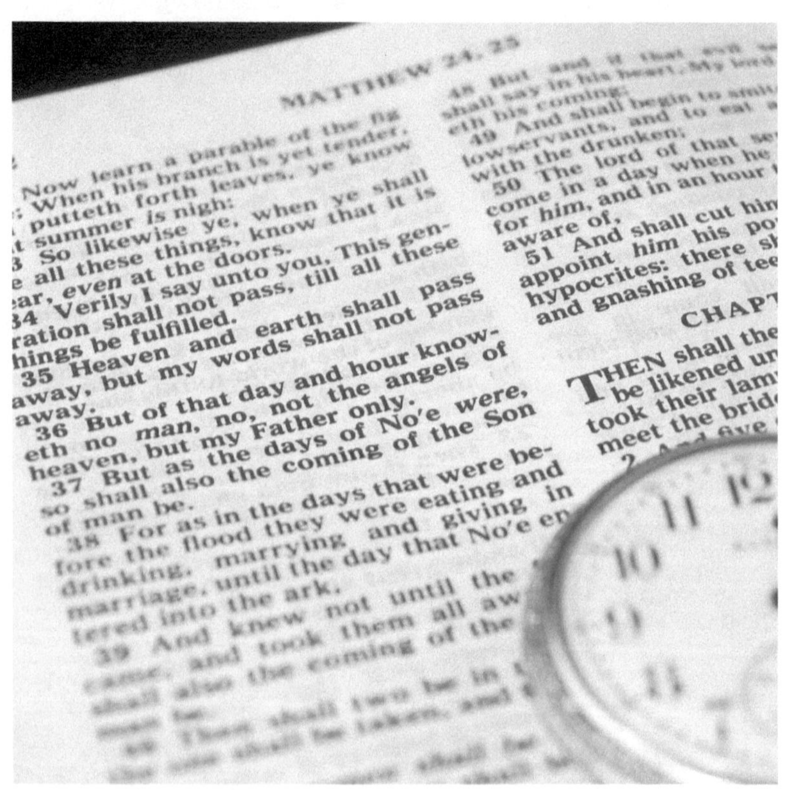

Colette opened her journal again and looked around the circle. "I was naturally confused by the whole idea of a second coming," she said. "I hadn't heard about it from my church, so I asked friends. One of them was very familiar with the subject. She told me Jesus would return one day, coming down from the clouds for the final and eternal judgment of all people. Some would be glorified, others punished.

"As I investigated religions after that, I discovered many traditions hold some version of this. Even Islam recognizes it. The Quran reads of Jesus: 'And His ˹second˺ coming is truly a sign for the Hour. So have no doubt about it, and follow Me. This is the Straight Path.' (Q. 43:61)."

Several eyebrows raised and a few head tilted nods revealed this was new information for the group.

"Jesus helped me understand it more clearly," Colette continued. "He directed me to the Bible."

She ran her fingers down the journal page before looking up again.

"He first pointed me to the prophet Daniel. You may remember Daniel survived the lion's den, but later he had a terrifying vision of four beasts ruling the earth until the Son of Man arrived in human form on the clouds of heaven."

She paused.

"Jesus explained it to me like this."

Colette read aloud.

"The four beasts Daniel saw represented four worldly kingdoms opposed to God. The fourth, Rome, was the most dreadful. Then YHWH, the God of Israel, took His throne, and the Son of Man was brought before Him. The Son of Man came to establish God's kingdom on earth. He was given everlasting dominion that will never be taken away.

"Jesus said, 'I am the Son of Man Daniel foresaw. My kingship cannot be destroyed.'"

The room was quiet. John felt as if the presence of God arrived with her words.

"After that," Colette said, "Jesus directed me to Matthew chapter twenty-four."

John leaned forward slightly while opening his Bible to the same.

"That's a passage about the end times." He said.

"Yes," she affirmed. "But listen carefully."

She returned to her notes.

"I met with my disciples at the Mount of Olives overlooking Jerusalem," Jesus said. "They were troubled about the destruction of the Temple and wanted to know when it would happen and how. They also asked about the signs of my coming."

Colette looked up.

"They still did not fully understand. They expected something dramatic," she said. "A political Messiah. A warrior king."

Carl nodded thoughtfully, recalling his studies. "That's exactly what people were hoping for."

"Yes," Colette replied.

She read again.

"Jesus shared, 'I warned them of the coming wars and false prophets. Many would rise claiming divine authority. I told my followers to watch for famines and earthquakes. These things had to pass."

She lowered the journal slightly.

"And… History shows that's exactly what happened."

John curiously asked, "What do you mean?"

Colette turned a page.

"That was my question too. Jesus shared that after his resurrection, men began appearing who claimed to be the Messiah. One was Theudas. Another was Judas the Galilean (not the betrayer). Later an Egyptian false prophet led thousands of followers into the wilderness and to the Mount of Olives. He claimed the walls of Jerusalem would fall at his command."

A man near the back shook his head.

"People believed that?"

"They were desperate," Colette said quietly. "They wanted someone to overthrow Rome and free Israel."

She glanced down again.

"Rome crushed those movements," Jesus said. "Hundreds and sometimes thousands of followers were killed or enslaved."

She looked around the room feeling tensions rising.

"Remember your breath." John said to the room. A collective and audible inhale and exhale queued Colette to continue.

"The tensions didn't stop there. Across the Roman Empire revolts and civil unrest grew more frequent."

She tapped the page. "Even the emperors played their part."

"Caligula," someone said.

Colette smiled. "Yes. Emperor Caligula ordered his statue placed inside the Jerusalem Temple."

"Bold move." Sarah said.

"Or stupid," her brother quipped.

John shook his head and reinforced, "That would have been unthinkable."

"It nearly started a war," Colette confirmed. "Only Caligula's assassination stopped it."

Sarah got up to refill her water from the pitcher in the corner. Ice clinked in the glass—the only sound for the moment.

Colette turned another page.

"But the unrest continued under Emperor Claudius when wars and rumors of wars were constant. Riots broke out between Jewish and Greek populations. Uprisings in Judea brought those false prophets mentioned; the ones promising divine deliverance."

Carl knew the story and added, "People still believed God would send a leader to overthrow Rome."

"Yes," Colette said softly. "That expectation never went away."

She took a slow breath and re-centered.

"Things escalated under the tyrant, Nero, with wars in the east and west. Grain shortages in Judea were severe. Relief efforts only temporarily aided the ravaging effects of earthquakes and famines. Grain from Egypt and figs from Cyprus fed Jerusalem's poor. But then catastrophe hit."

Outside, a truck shifted into a lower gear and faded. The lights overhead seemed to dim, as if the room itself had drawn closer to listen.

"What year was this now?" Sam's wife asked.

"Well, we're coming up on 66 A.D. All of this happened within forty years of Jesus' death and resurrection.

"Forty years. Huh... I never thought of that." Colette said. "As you all know, forty is used in the Bible to depict times of transformation. Good question. That's really remarkable."

The room murmured with that revelation, returning to stillness as Colette added to the weight of the story.

"In the year 66 A.D., Roman general Cestius Gallus surrounded Jerusalem, but then withdrew." Jesus said. "I had warned my disciples of all these signs so they would not be frightened. They recognized them and fled to the mountains east of the Jordan River. It was a good thing too, as the tribulation continued with Rome crushing Galilee, Parea, and Samaria before surrounding Jerusalem once again four years later."

She glanced down again.

John spoke softly. "The Christians escaped."

"Yes," Colette said. "But the city did not."

Her voice softened. "When Jesus showed me this next part," she said quietly, "it was more than words."

She emphasized, "He actually let me see it."

No one spoke as she recalled the sight.

"I saw the city surrounded. Roman banners filled the hills like a red ring around Jerusalem. Smoke rose from the outer gates. Nearly seventy thousand soldiers camped and fortified."

Her voice slowed.

"They were surrounding Jerusalem during Passover. The

year was 70 A.D. Hundreds of thousands of pilgrims were trapped inside the city walls."

She paused. A tear formed. It was real for her.

"Instead of uniting, three rival Jewish factions fought each other within those walls, burning grain stores and killing one another while the Romans encamped outside, waiting patiently for the turmoil to intensify inside.

"Mothers cried in the streets. By June the food was gone. The city devoured itself."

Her eyes lifted from the page.

"People starved. Families fought over scraps while some resorted to the unthinkable. Robbers searched homes, killing for food."

The breath had been taken out of the room. John broke the tension with a reminder to breathe, feel, and be present.

Colette continued, "Then the Romans breached the walls. Over one million people died and one hundred thousand enslaved."

No one moved. A moth tapped a light above and went still.

She closed the journal slowly.

"The Temple burned. When the fire subsided, Titus ordered the entire city and temple demolished. Not just destroyed, but laid even with the ground to prevent it ever becoming a fortress again. It happened just as Jesus foretold to His disciples (Matthew 24; Luke 21; Mark 13)."

After a moment she opened the notebook again.

"Do you see all these things?" Jesus said. "Not one stone will be left upon another. Also, as foretold, by the time the temple was destroyed most of the apostles and early disciples were handed over and killed. John was the only one to die of natural causes. With the collapse of Israel's religious and political order, the Temple system, priesthood, and sacrificial worship ceased.

"I then ascended in authority, enthroned as King after my resurrection and vindicated through the judgment on Jerusalem. Daniel and

Matthew depicted this as the Son of Man appearing, all the tribes of the earth mourning, followed by the Son of Man enthroned with power and great glory (Matthew 24:30).

'I became the new Temple and the prophecies were fulfilled. Following this, messengers were sent forth with the gospel, depicted as a great trumpet blast in scripture, gathering together the elect from every nation (Matthew 24:31)."

John leaned back in his chair. The wood creaked under him.

"So the second coming already happened?" John asked as he thought of God's earlier message of Jesus' return.

"Yeah, I have the same question." A voice from the third row echoed.

Colette met John's eyes.

"Yes, and..." she said, pausing. "That was only the first layer."

Colette rested her hands on the journal.

"Scripture often works in layers," she said. "Jewish teachers have understood this for thousands of years. The first layer is the plain meaning—the history itself. What actually happened."

She tapped the page lightly.

"That's what we've just been talking about. The Temple fell exactly as Jesus said it would."

She looked around the circle.

"But there are deeper layers too. Sometimes the text hints at something beyond the obvious. Sometimes the same words echo other places in scripture and open a deeper meaning. And sometimes—only after prayer and surrender—the Spirit reveals something mystical, something that cannot be seen with the mind alone."

John understood. "You're saying the prophecy was fulfilled… but not finished."

Colette smiled. "Exactly."

She lifted the journal again.

"History fulfilled the first layer. That first layer can even seem to repeat or rhyme throughout time. Perhaps it repeats until resolved in God's eyes. Have we not seen Israel surrounded by enemies, facing tribulation, and many predicting the second coming before? While those first layers provide insight, the Holy Spirit continues revealing deeper layers—ones that promise far more than most anticipate."

The room was silent until John asked, "What does that layer look like?"

Colette took her time, and with strength answered, "Christ emerging in union with you."

Some heads nodded in recognition. Others looked confused. Outside, dusk had thickened to dark. The windows held only the room's reflection now.

"Are you serious?" Maria asked, more curious than alarmed.

"Yes." Colette stated flatly. "Just as the people of Jesus' time were blinded by their desire for a Messiah to topple Rome, today's population is largely ignorant to this layer of the second coming."

John leaned forward. "Colette… if what you're saying is true… then what does the Second Coming actually look like?"

"God is King. God is the Lord. Christ emerges in a prepared *you*, perfected by the Holy Spirit. You are part of the return and you can choose to align with it or not."

She looked around the room and spoke with an invitation that sounded like a challenge, "Will you live as another Christ or resist and reject the power of the Lord another day, week, month, year, or lifetime?

"This is the way. If you want evidence, ask God to reveal the truth to you."

"What about the Antichrist?" A voice from the back called out.

"Good question. In this deeper layer of understanding, the Antichrist lives in us."

Now fully engaged, Sam asked, "In us?"

"Yes," Colette replied calmly. "It lives in every part of us where we block transformation in Christ."

"Block? How do we block it exactly?" He followed up.

"Oh let me count the ways." She smiled before rattling off a few, "Judgements, pride, unresolved emotional trauma, masks, out of alignment thoughts, words, and actions—some going generations deep.

Confused, Sam persisted. "But won't there be a powerful Antichrist leader who deceives nations before Jesus returns to defeat him? Then the dead will be raised… people will face final judgment… God will establish a renewed world where evil no longer lives."

Colette slowly rose to her feet, her cane forgotten for a moment. Her arms lifted in quiet praise. A smile crossed her lips, like an inside joke between her and God had found its punchline.

"Yes." She answered Sam with fervor. "But if you only look for this Antichrist in the world, you will miss the roots of it buried within you. After all, hasn't it deceived you? And won't Christ defeat it within you? And won't those parts of you, once dead, be raised for final judgment? The time is near for Christ's return. Until we address the parts deceived within us, the Antichrist lives. As the Antichrist dies in us, it will die in the world.

"The Antichrist is one who abandons Christ and makes that which is unlike Christ a priority. Look around. God is here in this room. God is alive in you, even if just as a pilot light on a stove. You are invited to be on fire for God."

She grabbed her cane, and walked a few steps to the center.

"Those in this fire will be softened, molded, and transformed into the shape needed for Christ to live and prepare the world for His full return at all levels of scriptural meaning. You are part of the answer God calls forth for the restored Kingdom. The new Jerusalem will arrive with each of you."

She paused.

No one spoke.

The room held silent. Colette stood strong, glancing down at her watch.

"Thank you all. I have shared enough today. If I don't leave soon, I'll be late getting home to Nashville. I'll return and visit with you again. Remember, most will look for signs and wonders, armageddon and the mark of the beast where he hasn't been. Look within first. Make your home ready. Then you will be prepared no matter the hour of Christ's return."

Colette thanked everyone for a lovely evening.

She took John's hand in both of hers as Celia gathered her bag.

"John, you are just as Celia described — warm, true, listening. Thank you for receiving me tonight."

She held his eyes.

"My first reason for being here is Jesus. He has work to do in the world, and some of us are here to make sure it reaches the people who need it. You are certainly someone I would trust with that work. I can see why He has trusted you. Would you let me tell a few friends about you?"

John's brow lifted. "Me? Of course. Tell them whatever the Lord moves you to tell."

She gently squeezed his hand.

"One more question while I have you," she said, eyes bright. "When do you think Jesus will return?"

The question hung between them. John didn't pause to think.

"Jesus is coming at this very moment."

Colette's smile reached her eyes. She nodded slowly.

"Yes," she said softly. "Yes, He is. Bless you, John."

He found himself thanking her again. "Colette, you opened my eyes tonight. Come back anytime."

"I'd like that," she said.

And then she was gone, Celia at her side, the door easing shut behind them.

The group quietly grappled with the immense challenge put

before them. If they were ready for more, all they needed to do was ask God for guidance.

After people left, and John turned out the lights, he returned to the story God had shown him earlier—the man named Jericho who had once prepared people for the return of Jesus.

For a moment he wondered if he was watching history begin to repeat itself.

CHAPTER 6
THE ACCIDENT

"For he shall give his angels charge over thee, to keep thee in all thy ways."
— Psalm 91:11

JOHN WOKE the next morning with a start.

In his dream he stood on a quiet seashore, collecting seashells. One shell caught his eye.

When he turned it over, a dark face stared back and said quietly, "You've opened a can of worms now."

Though unsettled, he tried to dismiss it as nothing—just another strange dream—but the image stayed with him throughout the day. The dreams returned the next night. And again the night after that.

After several days he stopped pushing them away.

A friend had recently messaged him about the power of dreams and invited him to an online interpretation group that met Wednesday evenings. John finally accepted the invitation.

When the group gathered online, he described his recurring dream. In the most recent version he found himself working as an engineer on a massive railroad project. His boss appeared and told him the train needed to move soon—people were anxious to travel and reach new lands.

Suddenly the train did something impossible.

It plunged beneath the ocean and traveled underwater, carrying people across the planet to their intended destinations —all in the blink of an eye.

When John finished explaining, the interpreter leaned forward and spoke deliberately. "There is a lot of meaning in this, John. The railroad project represents a pathway, or connection, being built between worlds. Between the human and the divine. Between separation and unity."

John listened carefully.

"As the engineer, you are the builder and bridge-maker. Someone who brings heaven's design into the world through vision, precision, and perseverance."

He paused and turned away. A dog had barked in the background.

"It's ok, hun. He can stay." He said to someone off camera.

The interruption allowed John to catch up on his notetaking.

"Ok, where was I…?" The interpreter asked. "Oh yeah, the boss. The boss represents divine authority—God or Christ—urging the work forward. The prompting isn't about haste or impatience, but about readiness. The world is prepared for what you are creating. People are waiting for it."

John felt his throat tighten, realizing this wasn't just a dream to sort out unconscious thoughts. This was a message… from God.

"The train traveling underwater is kind of a big deal," the interpreter continued. "It symbolizes moving through the depths of the unconscious, the spiritual realms beneath the visible world. Water, in scripture and dreams, can symbolize the Spirit, cleansing, and rebirth. The train moving beneath it suggests the path you're building does not fear those depths. It passes through the very waters that once separated humankind from God and transforms them into a means of travel."

The interpreter smiled gently.

"Just a second…" John said. He needed his brain to catch up with the details. "So the path I'm building… in the dream… connects people to the spirit realm?"

"Yes. And the train carrying people to new lands in the blink of an eye… that speaks to transcending time and space—Christ spreading through humanity… very quickly. Once the inner *track* within people is complete, outer movement, or changes are instantaneous; transformation will happen at the speed of divine will."

John's hand stilled. Paul the Apostle's words surfaced in his thoughts — *In the twinkling of an eye, we shall be changed.* He thought of the angle grinder. The cord that caught. The motor that died mid-air. That had been the same kind of speed.

The interpreter looked directly at John.

"The dream is encouraging your mission to support people completing the inner track for purification and alignment. This opens humanity to reestablish conscious union with God. Once that track is laid, transformation quickens for others without the struggles of earlier generations."

John thought of those who came before him. The saints, spiritual masters, and Jesus. Their sacrifices and wisdom had made it possible for John, a fourth-generation rural Kentucky guy, to even be in this position. *I'm certainly standing on the shoulders of giants,* he thought.

The interpreter stopped. A rare silence let the message permeate through the group. One of the participants unmuted, "Wow! John, if you indeed plan to help people build that inner *track,* I'd love to contribute. I just put my contact info in the chat."

John, too stunned to reply properly, simply said, "Thank you".

The call continued with another dream, but John didn't pay much attention. He turned the volume lower and sat quietly at his desk.

How could a simple dream contain something so complete?

This is too big for a machinist, he thought.

His head buzzed with energy. Something in his gut stirred. A wave of overwhelm. Questions of what to do next.

"God, are you there?" he asked aloud.

Through the dream and its interpretation, God had reached deep into John's psyche and switched something on.

As he reflected on the message, his phone rang.

The nurse's voice told him everything before she finished the first sentence. "Mr. Smith... your daughter... Sarah. She's been in a serious accident."

For a moment the sounds around him muffled, as if he were underwater. The world felt distant. She kept talking but the words failed to register.

First Janie, and now...

He stopped himself from finishing the thought.

"What hospital?" he asked, already reaching for his keys.

Hospital

The emergency room lights were harsh and unforgiving.

Sarah was alive.

But in a coma.

Her two girlfriends sat nearby, bruised and shaken but conscious. One of them explained what happened.

A semi-truck had suddenly swerved to avoid an object in the road. Sarah jerked the wheel instinctively, hit the median, and the car flipped several times before coming to rest upside down.

One of the girls wiped tears from her face.

"I know this will sound crazy, Mr. Smith. But I swear this next part is true." Her eyes opened wide.

"When the car stopped… Sarah wasn't breathing."

John's heart froze.

"And then her door ripped open," the girl continued. "A man… or something. pulled her out of the car and laid her gently on the road. He gave her mouth-to-mouth."

John leaned closer.

"But when the paramedics arrived," she whispered, "he was gone. He just vanished!"

John said nothing. His eyelids closed over tears of thanksgiving. He prayed for whoever had saved his daughter. He called friends and family to pray for a miracle.

The following days blurred together.

John slept in a stiff hospital chair beside Sarah's bed, waking every hour to check the machines. He held her hand, whispered prayers, and talked, believing she might still hear him.

Sitting beside her hospital bed, John opened his phone and stared at the last selfie she sent from the school parking lot.

Stephanie was overseas for work—frantic to get home.

When she finally arrived at the hospital two days later, John immediately saw the exhaustion in her eyes. Her hands were still trembling from travel as she dropped her bags and rushed to Sarah's bedside.

She kissed their daughter's forehead and closed her eyes.

John looked on in appreciation. Soon Stephanie looked up, holding Sarah's hand.

"Any updates?" She asked.

"None on Sarah." He said.

"What… What is it?" She asked seeing his jaw clench and eyes dart to the ceiling.

Then John told her what had happened the night before.

"Jesus spoke to me again." He hesitated.

"Do tell." Steph looked hopeful.

"He said, 'John, go to Mexico City. There is a Basilica you must visit. Go. You will find me there.'"

"When?" She asked.

"Now. But before you react…" he knew her disapproving look. "Jesus also said, 'I have everything under control. Sarah will live.'"

Stephanie stared at him in disbelief.

After rushing halfway across the world to be with Sarah, the last thing she expected was John leaving.

"You're serious?" she said.

John nodded silently.

Her frustration broke loose.

"What good does this do for Sarah?" she said, pacing beside the bed. "You going to Mexico?"

She stood, shaking her head.

"This is your daughter, John. Our daughter now."

Her voice cracked.

"I mean come on. Jesus sending you on a mission to Mexico? I need you here. Please stay."

John had no easy answer.

Later that night he walked alone to the hospital café.

The coffee tasted like metal.

He stood there staring at it, his mind torn in two directions.

Every instinct in him screamed to stay.

But the voice returned.

"John, it's time," Jesus said quietly. "Go to Mexico City. I will be waiting."

John closed his eyes.

"It's ok to cry, John. Let it out." the voice continued gently.

"But trust me now."

He had heard Jesus many times before in prayer. But never like this. This felt urgent. More of a command than invitation. Pressing.

Its urgency unsettled him. For the first time he wondered if exhaustion was playing tricks on his mind.

Am I losing it?

He sipped the coffee, and sat alone for a long time.

When he returned to Sarah's room, Stephanie was asleep beside the bed.

He kissed Sarah's forehead and then Steph's, before whispering,

"I'll decide in the morning."

John barely slept that night.

When he woke, the weight of obedience pressed on his chest.

Before leaving for the hospital, he packed a small bag.

Just in case.

As he backed out of the driveway, his phone buzzed.

A text from Stephanie:

> Go. Check your email. Your flight leaves in two hours.

> I may not understand this... but I trust your faith. I'll manage things here.

> I love you.

John stared at the screen.

His breath caught. He paused and closed his eyes with a slow breath. "Your will be done." He said. "Your will be done."

His eyes popped open. He was ready, grabbed the steering wheel and drove straight to the airport.

He made the flight with several minutes to spare.

CHAPTER 7
THE BASILICA

"Behold the handmaid of the Lord; be it unto me according to thy word."
— Luke 1:38

JOHN SPENT most of the flight staring at nothing, the low hum of the engines filling the cabin as he prayed under his breath. Every so often Sarah's face rose in his mind the way it looked in the hospital bed—still, pale, surrounded by wires and machines.

He clung to Jesus' words like a man clutching a rope in a flood, praying they were real.

Warm air embraced him as he stepped out of the terminal, thick with exhaust, travelers' voices, and the smell of street food from a nearby taco stand. Mexico City.

He grabbed a taxi straight from the terminal.

"Take me to the Basilica, please." John said, climbing in.

"Which one?" the driver asked.

John closed his eyes. Roses filled his mind—petals, dew, a fragrance he could almost smell. "I see roses," he said. "Is one related to roses?"

The driver glanced back in the mirror, his eyes brightening. "I know the one. We'll be there in thirty minutes."

The city rolled past—crowded streets, vendors, color and concrete. John prayed silently as they drove. *Lord, you said you'd be here. I'm here. Let this not be foolishness. Let this be you.*

"What do you know about this Basilica?" John asked.

The driver, a Hispanic man in his mid-fifties, looked at him again through the rearview mirror, eyes smiling.

"It is my favorite story of all time," he said. "Juan Diego, a farmer who converted to Christianity, was visited by the Virgin Mary on his way to Mass. It was December 9th, 1531. He heard beautiful music and a radiant voice calling him on Tepeyac Hill. Mary asked him to ask the local bishop to build a church on that spot. The bishop, understandably, asked for a sign. In response, Mary told Juan Diego to gather roses in his tilma."

"Tilma?" John asked.

"It's a cactus-fiber cloak. He did as Mary asked. Mind you, the roses were miraculously blooming in winter. When he opened the cloak before the bishop, the roses fell out, and an image of the Virgin Mary was imprinted on the fabric. That image is now the famous image of Our Lady of Guadalupe, still housed in the Basilica. It is one of the most visited religious sites in the world."

John hadn't heard the story before. He marveled at it and quietly hoped Jesus would provide a miracle for his daughter too. *Lord, you gave Juan Diego roses,* he thought. *I'm not asking for roses. Just my girl.*

They arrived at the plaza. As John stepped out of the cab Jesus whispered in his thoughts, "Meet in the back of the church." John froze for a moment, the words settling in his heart.

The driver pointed ahead. "Go to that one," he said, indicating a massive structure with a green copper roof draping down like a veil from its peak. John walked toward the new Basilica, built in 1976 after the old one became structurally unsound for the crowds.

"No, turn around," John heard Jesus say.

He stopped mid-step and turned. Past the old Basilica his eyes settled on a carillon shaped like a cross.

"That way?" he asked under his breath. Just then, the bells started ringing. He took that as a sign and walked toward the sound, passing the old Basilica, the new one now behind him. As he neared the carillon, his legs veered left as if an unseen force guided him.

As he circled toward the back of the carillon, a child's cry rang out. A young boy had fallen. No one seemed close by, so John jogged over. Just as he reached him, the boy's parents arrived and scooped him up.

"Go up the stairs," Jesus spoke again.

In front of John was a small building with a simple entrance. He stepped inside and climbed the stairs.

"You have found it," a woman said as he reached the top.

He stood in what was clearly an old chapel—simple and intimate. Seven wooden pews lined the center, two columns of chairs flanked them on either side, with narrow aisles between. An altar stood at the front. A small tour was underway.

"What have I found?" John asked his greeter.

The tall, slender woman, maybe twenty-five, smiled.

"This is the Old Parish Church of the Indians," she said. "It is the first hermitage built at the behest of Our Lady of Guadalupe. This is the sacred spot Our Lady's message to Juan Diego referred to—the church the bishop built. Come see. The old foundation is still visible."

She led John up to a stone archway to the right of the altar. Behind a museum-grade glass half-wall, he saw the remnants of the first church. Its fragile structure was supported by modern metal crossbeams to keep it from crumbling.

A wooden walkway for staff extended toward a beautiful image of Our Lady of Guadalupe—the original now enshrined in the new Basilica. Juan Diego, who had lived out his life in a hut next to the church, was buried there too.

The scene preserved what it might have looked like in the sixteenth century. The young woman—Cindy, he would learn—explained how this sacred little house on the plain of Tipalla became the foundation of a new creation, a catalyst for many coming to the Lord, changing hearts and birthing a new civilization of God's love in the region.

God had met the people through Our Lady of Guadalupe.

John thanked Cindy for the tour and walked down the right aisle to a back bench beneath a painting of St. Juan Diego receiving Mary. A few more visitors arrived and Cindy greeted them just as warmly, leading them toward the front.

"Ok, Jesus. I'm here. Now what?" John sat and let the question hang in the air. He felt uneasy. He had traveled all the way from Kentucky, left his daughter in a coma and his wife at her bedside.

His hands pressed into the worn wood of the pew as he repeated quietly, "Jesus, now what?" He scanned the room again. Seven pews. Two columns of chairs.

"God, are you there?" He asked.

Just then the chapel door opened behind him. A man hurried

in, looked immediately to his right, and came straight to John's bench. He smelled faintly of cigar smoke and expensive after-shave. He appeared to be of Italian descent. His legs were thick, his eyes dark. He checked his watch, breathing as if he'd run to get there.

He looked at John. "You John Smith?" he asked.

"Yes. How did you know?"

"Come with me," the man said, standing.

John caught his sleeve. "Wait. Who are you? Why do you know my name?"

"If you made it this far, you don't need to know my name," the man replied. "The guy who brought you also brought me." He winked and headed toward the exit.

John said a short prayer, stood, and followed.

"Let's take a walk," the man said once they were outside.

They followed a stone path past the beautiful Pocito chapel, which housed a spring believed to have miraculous healing properties. The trail wound past a green space abundant with rose bushes and eventually to the *sacred garden,* adorned with a large fountain and sculptures of indigenous people honoring the Virgin of Guadalupe.

Early in the ten-minute stroll, John asked, "Why am I here? What is your name? Who are you?"

"One at a time," the man said. "You'll get answers, John. Just not all of them today. I came here to invite you somewhere. It's confidential—a matter of national security. I don't expect you to believe me, but your path is about to change. I'm going to bring you to the White House for a special briefing with the President. And then, you'll have some decisions to make."

"Right. Ha. The President? Of the United States?"

"Yes, John."

"Me? I'm just a machinist and small-time minister from *Nowheresville, Kentucky,*" John said quietly.

"That's not for me to judge," the man replied. "It's your call. Or not."

John stopped walking. "What for though? I don't have any political background. Who are you again?"

"John, I can only tell you that you were sent by the same guy who sent me. Do you understand?"

"Jesus?" John asked. "You're saying Jesus sent you and sent me to meet in Mexico?"

"Yes."

"Why? Whatever for? I don't get it." John's thoughts spun ahead to a hundred scenarios.

The man stopped and turned toward him. "John, take this with you. It has everything you need." He pressed an envelope into John's hand. "It's been nice. I need to run. Keep your eyes on Mary."

He pointed ahead. They had arrived at the sacred garden's centerpiece—an image of Our Lady of Guadalupe raised on a rocky mound, her dark skin framed by a light blue cloak dotted with stars, radiant beams of gold spilling out around her. John took in the sight, the stones around her feet, the roses, the steady gaze.

"Am I not here, I who am your mother?" he heard.

"What?" John looked around for the source of the voice. The man was gone. No one else stood near him.

He turned back to the image. "Is that you... Mary?" he whispered.

"Am I not here, I who am your mother?" the voice repeated, gentle and firm at once. The garden was suddenly very still.

"Come to me. My son is with you. You are to serve God above all things. Remember this. I am visiting your daughter, and she will come home today. I am the way for her to find Christ. I am with her now. When you return, ask your wife to love you enough to trust Christ. Be at peace now."

John's knees gave way. He sank to the ground, overcome. It was the hug he had always wanted—the motherly love he longed for.

Something in his chest loosened and broke open. Tears came

with emotional waves. No more words or thoughts. Awe and gratitude filled his spirit.

When his breathing steadied again, he found his way back to the entrance. He prayed thanks, but the words felt too small. He felt like dancing. So light… full of grace.

He looked about, wanting to give something back to the place that had given so freely to him. He found an offering box and emptied all of his cash into it. It still didn't feel like enough, but it was what he had.

He excitedly explored the Basilica grounds, including the new Basilica able to hold ten thousand people for Mass—one of which was underway.

He attended, looking up in awe of the original tilma displaying Our Lady's image—an image scientists say should have disintegrated within decades—but it remains centuries later, surviving time, an acid spill and even a bombing.

Bells rang again across the plaza as he stepped outside. John, finally grounded, pulled out his phone and called Steph to share the good news.

"I don't think so, John," Steph said. "Sarah's still in a coma. She won't be coming home anytime soon. But you come home. It sounds like you got your message."

"I will," John replied. "I'll catch an early flight and be there mid-day tomorrow."

After the call, doubt crept in. *Had I made this all up? Was this some elaborate delusion?* He wondered if the trip was for some larger plan he couldn't yet see, or if he had simply lost his mind in grief.

That night he lay in his hotel bed and prayed the rosary for the first time in years. Bead by bead, the Hail Marys fell from his lips.

He then prayed, "God, if this is of you, guide me. I feel lost in this new world of revelation. If you want me to go to D.C., you will need to show me that Mary's message is true. I guess we'll see in the morning. Thank you for today. I put it all in your hands."

The next morning, John awoke to a text from Steph.

> You won't believe it. You simply won't believe it.
>
> We're home.

John's emotions overflowed in tears. Our Lady was right. Sarah was home.

He flew back, heart pounding the entire return trip. When he walked into the house, friends and family crowded the living room. Snacks covered the counters. Flowers filled every surface. His sister caught his eye across the room and pointed upstairs.

John took the stairs two at a time.

Sarah sat propped up in bed, color back in her cheeks. Steph sat beside her and leaped up to hug him as he entered.

"John, it's a miracle," she said, arms tight around his neck. "Can you believe it? She's home."

"How? How did this happen?" he asked, pulling back to look at both of them.

"As soon as we hung up," Steph said, "I heard a commotion in Sarah's hospital room. They wouldn't let me in, but it was clear she was coming out of the coma.

"When she woke and they finally let me see her, her first words were, 'We need to go home.' I told the doctors and they refused.

"While they were refusing, Sarah tried to sit up and nearly collapsed, but something steadied her. Slowly, she pulled the wires away, stood on shaking legs, and began dressing.

"'I'm going home,' she told the staff and started toward the exit. An orderly blocked her way. She looked him in the eyes and said, 'Move out of my way. I must go home now.'

"His eyes lifted over her head, like he saw something near

the ceiling, and he stepped aside. I tried to see what he was seeing, but there was nothing there.

Soon we were in the parking lot. Someone chased after us to sign a release, and here we are."

"Dad," Sarah said, patting the bed. "Come here."

John sat on the edge of her bed.

"I saw you," she said. "You were at the rocks talking with Mary. She stood right next to you. Her cloak was blue with stars. There was a big man with you. Mary told you she was with me. She was, Dad. Mary was with me. She said you were going to work in the White House and that I had to wake up and go home. That's when I woke up."

"White House? What's this about?" Steph asked, turning to John.

"I don't know yet," he said. "This guy…" He told them about the man in Mexico City, the envelope, the sacred garden, Mary's words.

Then he turned to Steph. "Will you love me enough to trust Christ?" he asked quietly.

She stepped back, eyes widening, as if something in her memory lit up. "This morning," Steph said, "I woke up at three a.m. to a woman's voice asking me those exact words: 'Will you love me enough to trust Christ?'"

John exhaled. "That is the question Our Lady told me to ask you."

Steph looked from John to Sarah and back again. "Then yes," she said slowly. "Yes, I will love you enough to trust Christ."

Her breath moved involuntarily as if being breathed, and her body shook slightly, like a person catching a chill.

Something in the room softened.

No one spoke.

The phone rang. Steph picked it up, listened, then held it out. "It's for you."

John curiously took the phone. "Hello?"

"It's time," came the man's voice on the other end. "I am

sending a car to pick you up. You're needed in D.C." The line went dead.

John stared at the screen. "Who was that?" Steph asked.

"The guy from Mexico City," John said. "He says I'm needed in D.C."

"That was quick. How long will you be gone?" she asked.

"I don't know," John said. "It's all very cryptic. All I have is in this envelope. He's sending a car now. I need to pack."

He handed the envelope to Steph. She opened it. Inside was a hand written note on official White House stationery signed by the President:

John, There are moments in history when what is required of a man is not preference, but necessity.

We find ourselves in such a moment.

I have been made aware of you... though not in a way that can be easily explained. That alone is enough for me to take this seriously.

I would like to meet you. Come prepared to speak plainly.

K. I. Tchi

The pace of John's life quickened. His flight to D.C. gave a much needed chance to check in with God.

"God, are you there?" John opened a notebook with pen in hand. Just as before, God wrote with him. The first time writing with God had been confusing. Now it felt natural. The words came faster over the years. The lessons deepened.

"God, I don't understand. Why am I going to D.C.? What do you want from me there?

"John, you are given a mighty mission in support of my vision for humanity. It is just a small detour from where you thought you were going. You'll like it. Be present. Feel the man that you have become. I am pleased with you. I am where you are. We walk as one."

John opened his eyes. Warmth rose in his heart. He would go forth in mystery to the unknown with faith—where he was headed was of Christ.

"Thank you. I love you, God." He quietly repeated "I love you, God" over and over until the plane landed.

CHAPTER 8
D.C.

"He hath put down the mighty from their seats, and exalted them of low degree."
— Luke 1:52

John arrived at the White House on a quiet morning—eerily quiet, the kind of stillness John cherished at 5 a.m. on Saturdays at his machine shop.

The South Lawn stretched out behind iron fencing and armed guards, the early sun catching the white columns of the Executive Mansion.

John stood for a moment taking it in. *I don't belong in places like this,* he thought. *Wow.*

After clearing Secret Service screening, a White House Military Aide met him with clipped formality and led him through a series of corridors that smelled faintly of polished wood and fresh paint.

In the Roosevelt Room he signed confidentiality paperwork and sat through a video he barely absorbed. He was more captured by the equestrian Rough Rider portrait of Roosevelt hanging over the mantle.

What he felt, more than understood, was that he had stepped over a threshold. This was no longer about Mexico, or even Sarah. He felt like a *part* being prepared in God's *machine shop.* Despite how strange it all felt, he reminded himself to trust.

He was ushered to a side room for a polygraph. The technician asked questions in a tone nearly bored; John answered honestly. Afterward, alone again, he waited. His breath steadied only when he whispered a small prayer: *Jesus, go before me. I'm yours.*

An hour passed before another aide appeared. "The President will see you now."

John stepped into the Oval Office and felt the weight of history pressing quietly around him. The Italian man from Mexico sat on a couch—legs thick, posture coiled, watching him without expression. A single nod when their eyes met.

Behind the Resolute Desk, President Tchi was on a call. He raised a finger—*one moment*—and gestured toward a chair near the Italian. John sat. He tried not to stare at the man who had somehow known his name two thousand miles ago.

"Thank you, Mr. President. I'll be in touch within the hour," President Tchi finally said, hanging up. He stepped around the desk and greeted John with surprising warmth.

"You must be the 'John' I've heard so much about."

"It's an honor, sir," John replied, rising.

"John," the President said, settling into his chair, "I have a very important job that needs your attention. I want you to head up my spiritual council."

"Your… what?" John asked.

"My spiritual council. A circle of leaders from every major religion. I want you to lead it."

"Is this something new, sir?" John asked, unfamiliar with the term.

"Every president has policy advisers. Some have economic councils. A few have had informal faith advisers. What we're building goes further."

The President gestured toward the ceiling as if referring to rooms beyond the Oval Office, or perhaps the heavens.

"The framework is already forming. Rabbis, imams, priests, monks, philosophers—faith leaders from around the world. But they need someone at the center. Someone who isn't political."

His eyes settled on John.

"Someone who listens."

John blinked. "This is an honor, sir. This is quite sudden for me. I'd like to pray on it."

"Naturally. But don't take too long. There is work to do." The President seemed confident John would say yes, even after prayer.

John closed his eyes for a moment and asked the Holy Spirit to guide him. His hosts gave him space with their patience.

An inner prompt came forth in a question. "Sir… why me?"

The President didn't hesitate. "John, we're living through an unprecedented moment. Never has the world been so close to destroying itself. Physical threats have diminished, sure. But now… the rebuild is critical. Peace… it's still fragile. We need Christ in the mix—no, in the center."

He leaned in. "You have proven worthy of the task… at least according to the visions my staff received."

John shook his head. "Sir, we just met. I only spoke with this gentleman—" he nodded to the Italian—"for a few minutes. On what basis…?"

John rubbed his palms together unconsciously, the way he did before activating a new machine.

"Jesus," the President said plainly.

For a heartbeat John wasn't sure if *Jesus* was an expletive or an answer. Then he saw the President's expression.

"Excuse me?" John whispered.

"It's simple," the President said. "Jesus has shown five members of my staff your face. You're the one."

The words landed like a bell in John's chest. Not loud—just undeniable. He took a slow breath. *Lord, if this is you…*

The Italian man finally spoke. "You had a visitor recently—Colette Jembowski. Remember?"

"Of course. Celia's mother."

"She wasn't there by accident, John. Even though your face had been shown to us, we had someone we trusted visit you in person." He paused, letting that settle. "Colette raved about you. Do you remember what she asked when she left?"

John frowned, searching. There had been so much happening that night. He closed his eyes. "She asked when I thought Jesus would return."

"And what did you say?" the Italian pressed.

"I said… Jesus is coming at this very moment."

The Italian nodded once. "That was our code. Given to each of the five, along with a mental image of your face. It is time, John. Jesus is coming. And now you have a choice."

John remembered Colette's hands holding his — the way she'd said her first reason for being at Old Hickory that night was Jesus. He had believed her then. He still believed her . Yet, the mission was larger than he realized—perhaps than she realized too.

The President leaned back, studying him. "We wish to align in Christ as a nation. We want to choose rightly consistently. We are saying 'yes' to Jesus at the highest level of government."

The Italian continued, "Your appointment is part of that yes. He's here, John... in the White House. God is with all of us. We were invited—no, warned—to create a prayer circle, a fortress of divine love to guide each and every member of our nation's leadership. President Tchi takes this seriously. Your role will complete our defense—and help us revamp our offense in the spiritual sense. You will guide the heart of this nation."

"You will have everything you need to do this well," the President reinforced. "Resources, security, staff. Jason will walk you through the details."

Jason Slock, the Italian, nodded. "Compensation, housing in Washington, travel, protection for your family — all of that will be arranged. Build the team you need. We'll vet them. If you accept, you can be operational by week's end."

Jason spread his hands. "What do you say?"

John felt his pulse in his throat. He glanced at the President and back at Slock, studying the soldier-like stillness, the steady eyes, the posture that never seemed to relax.

Something about him stirred a memory.

From television. Late-night briefings during the war years, a calm voice explaining the inexplicable to a nervous nation.

Jason Slock. The Secretary of Defense.

A man who did not fly to Mexico City for small reasons.

John's stomach tightened.

Jason clarified. "John, if it helps your decision, your compensation includes three million a year, Secret Service protection for your family... many benefits. This will be good for you."

"Three million?" John said, digesting the number. His machine shop's best year barely cleared three hundred thousand.

President Tchi raised one eyebrow as he nodded to John, knowing full well the amount offered was significant.

They weren't messing around, and did not want money to be an obstacle. Something holy and dangerous was unfolding. Something real.

The realization humbled John. These men were moving with the seriousness of people who knew something he didn't.

John swallowed. "Sir… can you tell me what I'm getting myself into? Who had this position before me, and why is it vacant?"

Jason leaned forward slightly. "Some people here think you're a miracle," he said evenly. "Others think you're a security risk."

The words landed harder than John expected.

The President's expression gentled, the weariness of office surfacing through the cracks of confidence. "No one had it before you, John. There is no precedent for what we're building."

He moved to the window, hands clasped behind his back. "The world is trying to rebuild after the war. But the financial battles continue." He looked out over the South Lawn as if searching for language that wouldn't shatter something fragile.

"China unified the world's financial systems after the sovereign-debt collapse. As you know, nearly every nation fell. Ours included." He exhaled. "We're barely learning to stand upright, like a wounded animal regaining its legs. People are angry, scared. The mental health pandemic left a deep scar. The nation is balancing on a tightrope."

He turned back to John. "We need spiritual clarity. Not politics. Not strategy. Clarity."

Jason leaned forward, resting his forearms on his knees. "You complete our defense, John—at least the part that matters most. The spiritual architecture of a nation. You'll guide us, and bridge leaders from every faith tradition. Help us see through deception. Help us act rightly."

The President added, "If it goes well, we avoid another war. If we fail..." He didn't finish.

John felt something move in him—not fear, not pride, but a deep and trembling quiet. Almost a bowing of the soul. *Lord, this is a lot. Guide me.*

His doubts whispered: *I'm not trained for this. I'm not political. I'm just a dad, a husband, a guy from Kentucky passionate about God.*

But beneath the doubt rested another truth: the unmistakable sense of being carried.

John looked from the President to Jason, then back again.

The room waited.

He surrendered to faith, to Christ... and stood.

"Mr. President... I don't know exactly what I'm saying yes to. But if Jesus is calling me to this, and evidenced by a recent miracle or two he is, then you can count on me."

The President's shoulders dropped in relief. "Good. Then it's settled."

Jason rose too, the soldier in him honoring John's decision. "We'll get you home. Speak to your wife. Bring her into the fold. We need you steady, John. We need your whole life aligned to this."

He paused. "And understand something — not everyone in this city will welcome this."

John nodded, heart pounding. "Understood."

"If you do your job well," the President said, "for the first time in a long time, we'll lead from the soul."

John glanced once more around the Oval Office — the desk where wars had been decided, the chairs where history had turned.

For a strange moment he wondered what it would feel like to carry the weight of this room every day.

On his own, he had no business standing there. Only of and with God did any of it make sense.

John offered a small, reverent smile, and shook their hands. "Then let's get started."

CHAPTER 9
JESUS TAKE THE WHEEL

Trust in the Lord with all thine heart; and lean not unto thine own understanding."
— Proverbs 3:5

THREE MONTHS LATER, John returned to the White House with a bone to pick. He had felt frustration and needed clarity. Something the President had promised to lean into had been set aside. It was time to revisit it.

An aide met him at the door of the Oval. "The President will see you now."

Inside, President Tchi rose quickly, relief brightening his tired features. "John, you're doing it. By George, you're actually doing it." He motioned him closer. "Sit. I need to prepare you for something."

John took the seat opposite him. He could feel it—the air charged the way it gets before a storm.

"We're hosting a world summit," the President said, hands laced together. "Leaders from around the globe. If our intelligence is accurate, several of them are infected with a spiritual *virus* of sorts. It's something dark, a deception that's taken root in their souls."

He swallowed. "I need you and your team there. Can you identify it live, in real-time and address this *virus* in the moment?"

John breathed deeply as he centered. "Mr. President, I like our chances. Jesus is at the helm. But you can't walk into a meeting like that unprepared. We need to finish the work we started last month. You need your fortress clear."

The President leaned back, exasperated. "I thought... maybe... you could just do it for me. Handle the spiritual side yourself."

John shook his head gently. "You can't have me breathe for you, walk for you, speak for you, or do this for you, sir. Only you can align your soul... with God of course. Anything else is temporary. Spiritual shadow-work, not transformation."

The President winced. "You're saying I've been avoiding my part."

"I'm saying your nation needs you awake," John replied. "And awakening is not something anyone can delegate."

Realizing he'd spoken more sharply than intended, he softened his tone. "Sir, Scripture tells us that without wise leadership, a nation will fall. I just want you at your best. All of us need to be aligned."

President Tchi nodded, shame and resolve traveling across his face. "Alright. Tonight. Six o'clock. Join me for dinner. Bring your wife. Let's do this right."

Steph flew in just in time for dinner. They all wore casual clothes—casual for the White House, anyway—and were welcomed as unofficial guests of the President that night. Steph had brought Sarah along, and the President had brought his son, James—both now eighteen.

The moment they sat down, Steph lit up the room. She always had that effect—sharp-minded, compassionate, unafraid to challenge assumptions.

The President admired her for it. His wife had passed during his first term, and something about Steph's wit and clearheaded warmth reminded him of the woman he loved.

"So, Steph," he began, "what do you think of all this nonsense in Cambodia?"

Steph didn't miss a beat. "Besides their authoritarian tactics to suppress voting and keep power in the family? Disgusting. Their human rights violations are unimaginable. They're in China's pocket while pretending to be our ally. That puts us—and everyone else—on a collision course. The real question is, what is the U.S. willing to do about it?"

The President laughed through a grimace. "Well said. Exactly what my advisors should be saying. John, what about you?"

John lifted his water glass, choosing his words. "I stay out of politics, sir. But I lean toward peace—real peace, not just the absence of conflict.

"If we want lasting stability, we should work with grassroots groups, not just governments. Build reconciliation efforts from the ground up. Fund memory initiatives. Heal generational wounds. Any solution that ignores trauma will fail."

The President stared at them both, almost amused. "You two surprise me. Steph, I could put you in charge of half the State Department. And John—'I stay out of politics,' huh? You sound like you've been preparing for the job without knowing it."

John smiled. "We just know the region, sir. Family ties through marriage. You picked a topic we've talked about for years."

"Well," the President said, leaning back, "between the two of you, I see a political future forming. Interested?"

John shook his head gently. "Not in the traditional sense, sir. We're here for what God asks of us. And I believe we have actual work tonight—remember?"

That redirected the moment. The President nodded. "Yes. You're right."

To make space for the heavier conversation, he turned to the teens.

"Sarah, James—how about a movie? The newest Bond."

James blinked. "It's not out for months!"

The President grinned. "We have it early. Though I'm not as involved any longer, Neal Purvis wrote many of the Bond movies and got his hands on the latest for us to check out."

James shot up from the table. "Yes! Sarah, wait till you see the theatre. They renovated it when the State Ballroom was added. You'll feel the movie in your bones."

Sarah followed, more interested in spending time with James than the Bond movie. She gave her father a small wink—the one that said *I'll behave, don't worry*. She knew he was sensitive about her being alone with boys.

When the teens left, the air shifted.

"Alright, John," the President said. "Down to business. What's needed here?"

John took a breath. The Holy Spirit pressed gently on his chest, the kind of nudge he recognized as guidance. "Three things, sir."

The President straightened.

"First," John said, "we revisit the healing we began around your wife's passing. You opened a door then. We need that door opened again and mourn properly."

The President exhaled slowly. "I remember. I saw her… just for a moment when we did that exercise. Surrounded by angels. I felt at peace for the first time in years. I even had a couple dinner dates this past month and was able to stay focused on my date instead of arguing in my head about how I was betraying or not betraying my marriage. It's been helpful. I'm thankful, John."

"Good," John said. "That peace matters. It is not finished though. There's more to resolve. Otherwise, someone can weaponize it against you."

John continued. "Second, you need to understand the spiritual landscape. Some of the global leaders have shields—illusory tricks to deceive. What appears to be true on the surface may not be the truth beneath. You must learn to see the forest beneath the ocean."

Steph's brow furrowed slightly. "Meaning?"

"Meaning," John said, "these leaders may believe their own illusions, or someone may be projecting them intentionally. Discernment is everything."

The President pressed his palms together. "And the third thing?"

"We tune your hearing to recognize God's divine signature," John said. "So you can distinguish Jesus' voice from the others."

The President swallowed. "Is that even possible?"

"It's the reason I'm here," John said.

Silence draped the room for a moment.

John pressed forward. "Mr. President, imagine each global leader carries an illusion — a surface picture that hides what is actually underneath. If a leader's surface shows an ocean, but the truth beneath is a forest, we must see through to the forest."

"Should I even be here for this part?" Steph questioned.

"You have all the proper clearances. Stay, Steph," the President responded.

John continued. "Most likely the leaders are unconscious of the shields and believe the illusion is their reality."

"So they think the *ocean*, in your metaphor, is true and not the *forest* it covers up?" the President asked.

"Possibly. Some may have someone like me on their team. If so, those leaders could intentionally project the ocean as a shield to mask the truth and deceive others.

"Today, we'll activate your divine signature to see as Jesus informs. I will guide you to maintain clear sight and conscious awareness of when you are ON-target and when you are OFF-target. Fair?"

"Couldn't Jesus guide me directly?" the President asked.

"Yes, if you allowed him to speak to you, but you are blocking His messages."

"So, operator error on this *device*?" He humbly patted his chest a couple times.

"Exactly. But that's what we are here to correct. If we can get you to do both—If you can see through those ocean shields to the forests, AND listen to Jesus, heaven will make a home in you, and we are in great shape. In fact, only God's will can be done from there on out. Let's start by making sure you can discern between the illusory shield and what's true."

John and the President went to work. The Holy Spirit guided John, and with each step the power of Christ was more visible in President Tchi. His personal transparency and trust in John quickened the process. Soon, they applied the President's new skills on several issues.

"Let's examine congress," John said. He brought out a photo —a humanitarian trip congressional leaders recently took to Russia.

"Now, look at one person in particular. I want you to pay attention to congresswoman Ariel. Say out loud, *I cancel my need to know anything about her.*" He did.

"Now say, *I release controlling any part of her.*" He did.

"And now say, *I allow Jesus to inform me of what I need to know right now.*" He did. "Now, listen in your heart, breathe, and watch what arises in you. Thoughts, images, feelings, anything."

The President closed his eyes.

A long moment passed.

"Nothing," he said.

John nodded calmly. "That's alright. Your mind is still trying to control the process. Before we do it again say, *I release control of the process,* and breathe."

A big sigh and release followed the President repeating the statement. John and Steph sat in silence, breathing with him as he centered.

The President had struggled like this during their earlier sessions as well. Letting go of control never came easily to him, but he was willing.

Once ready, he continued the exercise, *"I let go of any judgments held for or about Ariel."*

The President's demeanor changed after that one.

"And once again," John prompted. *"I allow Jesus to inform me of what I need to know right now."*

Tchi repeated it. They quietly waited.

"I got something. I think I got something." The President said with excitement.

"Great, what is it?"

"I saw Ariel and light… it sharply cut through her and inside

I saw darkness. It glittered like the inside of a gemstone. Amethyst perhaps. That was it. Amethyst."

"Great. Perfect. Amethyst in scripture symbolizes wisdom, clarity and purity. That's a good sign. This signifies that Ariel is someone you can trust. Metaphors are a common mechanism for spiritual insight. They could include everyday objects or out of this world metaphors. God will use whatever mechanism possible to get to a person He's calling.

"Now that we know she's a *good egg,* the next stage is to access any messages about her. So ask, *Jesus, what is it I most need to be aware of about Congresswoman Ariel?*"

He asked and waited for an answer. This was the hard part for most people—patience. People get distracted, anxious, and feel pressure to come up with something.

The reality is letting go in full surrender is the only way. Presence is necessary when praying. The President knew this and cancelled his goal to figure it out, maintained conscious breathing, felt his emotions, and awaited an answer.

His face suddenly expressed joy with a big inhale, eyebrows up and mouth curling at the edges. "I got it. She's partnering on a deal with Jeremiah Diggs. They need my help. I can bring Russia to the table on minerals needed for the efforts. I didn't know any of that before, but now it's so obvious. I can't believe I missed it."

"Right on, Mr. President. You stayed in sync and aligned. You can trust this message. The metaphorical *ocean* gave way to the forest below. You've dismantled the false narrative, and see the truth."

"I like this. Can we do more?" the President asked.

John confirmed. "We will do more, yes. Remember, this only works if you stay connected to God. That's where the insight comes from. That is how this message came to you.

If you try to use it for your own gain, unaligned with God's will, you'll drift off course. You want to maintain God at your center. That is always first and foremost. The Holy Spirit will correct you when you're off and retrain you. That's how we learn to live as Christ."

"This is your path, Mr. President. And as our nation's leader, it is the reason America will thrive. Where past leaders were easily deceived, you'll expose the truth in the light. My team and I will support you and all in the administration, but they won't all make it."

"That's a sobering thing to say."

"It is, but takes work—and not all are willing."

"John, is there an end to this, a finish line so to speak, where a person is perfected?"

"I believe so, Mr. President. I believe we will do this until the last judgment." John said.

"The last judgment?" President Tchi leaned in, well aware of its Biblical references.

"I remember this one… did a paper on it in school. Paul in 2 Corinthians 5:10 shares that we must all appear before the judgment seat of Christ and make amends for what we do in the body, whether good or evil."

"Yes, the last judgment." John adjusted himself in his seat knowing what he said next would likely conflict with Tchi's understanding of the last judgment.

"Mr. President, the Lord taught me that it works like this. When one surrenders to the Holy Spirit he'll be led to restoration. It is a process that releases the effects of sin, and teaches the person how to live righteously. Those who do this eventually are born into new life. They transform and begin to live as Jesus did —aligned with God. And, in Christ they will not taste the second death referenced in Revelation.

"You see, they make amends for every sin through the process and the process is completed at the last judgment, when nothing remains to separate them from God. Their name is in the book of life. They are in pure alignment as one with God."

"But I thought the last judgment would come at the end of the world," the President said.

"It does. That is the end of the world, Mr. President. Heaven makes a home in the purified soul, and the world loses its power over that person. The kingdom of God begins to live within them, and the life of Christ becomes visible through their walk in the world. That person becomes a Christ in full bloom so to speak—one with God, living in heaven while still on earth."

"Wait a minute. This is a lot to take in, John. I was anticipating an armageddon. Are you saying that is not what the end of the world means?" President Tchi looked down and shook his head in disbelief. "What if you're wrong, John?"

"If I am wrong, then anyone who follows this way will live as a Christ and the world will still end. But what if I am right, Mr. President? What if we are both right?"

Tchi thought for a moment—looked at Steph who had heard all this before. She was smiling… waiting for it to land fully in the President.

Finally, he smiled turning back to John. "If you are right, John, then we must make this the utmost priority, for we are not destroying a planet, we are transforming a planet to be whole with God. That changes everything.

"The world at war would die as humanity leans in on living —as more Christs emerge. Everything would change."

He repeated. "I'm seeing it, John. We have nothing to lose and everything to gain. If Christ is our judge and we address our sins while in a body, we open to heaven right now. And whoever lives in Christ would naturally treat others as if he or she were also Christ."

"Exactly," John emphasized. "Remember Jesus saying, *as you did it to one of the least of these my brothers, you did it to me*? So, to answer your question, Mr. President, every end is just a new beginning.

"The path is not to achieve an end. It is to live eternally as one in being with our Creator."

The room went quiet. A knock at the door. A woman brought in coffees and some light desserts.

"Thank you, Darla," Tchi said.

Darla set down the tray. She and Tchi shared a quick smile, the easy kind that comes from years of small interactions."

When she left, John sipped his coffee and said, "It is time to get back to work, for right now you have a job to do. If you do it well, many lives will turn to Christ. If you fail, then God will have to find another way. Shall we continue?"

"Yes," Tchi said as he lightly slapped the table for emphasis.

CHAPTER 10
SEE THE FOREST

"What I tell you in the darkness, tell in the light; and what you hear whispered in your ear,
proclaim on the housetops.
— Matthew 10:27

PRESIDENT TCHI and Steph barely had their first bite of dessert before John kicked things off again.

"OK. Let's continue. Say, *Thank you Jesus for this insight on Ariel and Jeremiah. Is there anyone else to focus on?"*

President Tchi did this and soon described an image appearing in his mind's eye, "I see Russia."

"Great!" exclaimed John. "Sounds like we are moving on to global leaders. Imagine President Putin and ask Jesus the following question, *Is there anything I am to know about Putin?"*

He asked and soon shared, "I see him on a frog traveling on the ocean. He looks good for his age. He's wearing a wetsuit. He just dipped under, swimming to the bottom of the ocean.

"He's opening a hatch down there and swimming through. Ok, he closed the hatch and the water is draining. He's in an airlock, taking off the wetsuit. Underneath, he's dressed in a suit and tie. He steps through another opening into a conference room. He's alone. No, wait. People are arriving. I see the leaders of China, North Korea, India, and more entering the room. Putin is sitting with them now.

"I see a 3-D model on the table and images of rare earth minerals. The model shows a city with buildings I don't recognize. Country flags dot the model. Is this some sort of global alliance?

"China is leading the meeting. He's speaking in Chinese but I can understand him in English. They say they must protect themselves from the unpredictability of the West."

Tchi's eyes squinted as if reading. "They're building a system that doesn't need us. They don't know what to do with us. They are reviewing a map of proposed trade routes... and the United States is not on it. Do they plan to isolate us from trade? Wait. There's a timeline on the wall. Long. Decades. Maybe longer."

President Tchi's face looked ashy. He leaned back slowly in his chair, eyes still closed, as if trying to hold the images steady in his mind. They arrived faster than they had in previous sessions.

"Mr. President," John said gently. "Ask if this has happened yet."

He did.

The answer came instantly: "Yes. It happened years ago."

For the first time, John understood that the work God began in that hickory church in Kentucky would have massive international implications.

"This, Mr. President, is why we do this work. You want insight. You're getting insight—information that will help you respond instead of getting blindsided later. Now, pretend you just heard about this in the mainstream news. What would you do in response?"

"I'm fuming, John. They have no right. It's uncalled for. This is ridiculous. After what we did to calm the storm following Europe's collapse. They are retaliating from the mistakes of my predecessors. We must change this."

"No," John retorted. "You are angry. This is exactly the type of energy people before you acted from. Instead, I invite you to do it differently. You can. But first, we must address the anger."

"Come on John. You're testing me here. I want to get on the phone and make some moves."

"Don't sir. Please." John said. President Tchi looked at Steph and could see she agreed with John.

"Ok. What should I do?"

"Breathe and let the anger be felt fully."

The whole room shifted energetically as his anger surfaced more and more. He tried breathing but would get lost in his rage.

"I want to control those sons of bitches and break up their alliance."

"Breathe," John reminded him. "Why do you want to control them and break this up?"

"Are you kidding? If I don't, they'll lead the world and the US will fall behind."

"And if we fall behind?" John asked.

"The world will laugh at us. They'll laugh at me. I'll preside over the fall of our nation just as we are getting back on our feet. And these yahoos will control us."

"And?" John asked.

"Are you kidding? I can't stand for that. My name will be marred. I need to get in front of this. Fudge!"

But he didn't say fudge.

John leaned forward.

"Mr. President, before you solve the nation's problems, you must address what is happening in you."

He held the President's gaze.

"You must address what's in you first… before action."

The President's eyes opened wide. He nodded and took a few more breaths. He was getting it.

John continued. "You are now seeing beneath your own ocean, your own deception… to the forest below. Can you see that? You're poking at the hidden parts. If you don't address them, your enemies coming to the Summit will see them and use them against you."

He paused.

"Are you game?"

"Yes."

"Ok. Repeat after me, *I can't do this alone. I allow Christ to be here right now. Holy Spirit, guide me through this moment.*"

President Tchi repeated the phrases.

"And now say: I GET to be in this position. I GET to feel what I feel. I accept responsibility for our nation. I accept allowing Christ into our nation at all levels. I invite Jesus to speak."

He followed the prompts and waited. His neck muscles tightened, but he noticed and breathed into them. His face contorted as if he were looking at something, watching a scene unfold in his mind.

President Tchi then broke the silence. "I got it. Jesus is telling me to go to the meeting and lay our cards on the table. He says not to hide the way we have in the past. He's showing me how to navigate the room. I start with Germany. Then, I go to Italy and France. Canada followed by Mexico. I see all these leaders combining into one force and the force comes to grips with the truth. We made mistakes. Now it's time to admit them and open a dialogue for change."

"How do you feel about that?" John asked.

"Peacefully uncomfortable. I don't see how those nations will agree or why those nations in that order in particular. What do I do with this? Are these metaphors or are they to be trusted ideas?

"Ask."

"How?"

"Say, *God I see these leaders and countries. What are they for?"*

He asked and heard, "I am with you. Go forth and do this. Trust the person you are becoming, not who you have been. You and I are one on this. Trust."

And with that the President teared up saying. "I've never felt this close to God in my life. I feel he's in me. How did you do this?"

John smiled, "I didn't, Mr. President. God did it."

"But how did this start for you?" Tchi asked him.

"Well, it started with an angle grinder." He told the story. "From there, I was taught a few things by worldly teachers until God showed up in some special ways.

"I learned that of myself, without God, I am nothing. Only with God is this restorative process possible. Whether you believe the Bible to be true or just parables, the story of Adam and Eve requires reconciliation with our Creator.

"Jesus gave us everything we need for that reconciliation. The Holy Spirit will guide anyone and everyone who opens to that support.

"Our physical systems—body, mind and spirit—must be retrained, re-tuned, and purified to have this process complete. It's a process. It always works. As you can see, it requires practice, sir. It requires discipline. Your faith will grow. Trust the process."

"It's a lot to ask of an old codger like me, John. But I'm willing."

"And for that I am grateful." John said. "For the first time in my lifetime, Mr. President, I feel as if we have a shot at turning our nation around and restoring it to a Christ-centered country.

"Our best days are ahead of us if collectively we choose to do this. It is not a religion. It's a relationship. All the glory goes to God.

"If we don't do this, God has shown me a dire future with many hardships and continued loss of freedoms. We must stay aligned and enroll our allies and our people. It is God's plan. You are the hands and feet of Christ right now, and you are not alone."

CHAPTER 11
THE SUMMIT

"For many are called, but few are chosen."
— Matthew 22:14

By early March of 2034, delegates from one hundred fifty-six countries had arrived in Washington. It was the largest gathering of world leaders ever to visit the White House. Much of the city was closed to the public. Security was immense. The skies were watched, the streets controlled, the perimeter layered with protection meant to both reassure and intimidate.

The morning of the summit began with ceremony. There was a parade, a brief concert, and an exhibition soccer match with athletes from a dozen nations playing together for the visiting heads of state. The whole thing was meant to signal cooperation, recovery, and hope after the war years.

John was not at the parade.

He was in a secured side room at the White House with several members of the spiritual council and a handful of trusted intercessors from different faiths, praying over the day. Their assignment was simple: Pray to God, listen, and obey.

The room had been peaceful, harmonious. Private prayers. Group-led meditations. Plus, for every person in the room, five more were positioned strategically across the city, covering it in prayer.

A spiritual battle. A weapon of some sort. No one knew, but something had abruptly changed. A woman stopped mid-prayer and opened her eyes.

"I don't like this," she said softly. "Something bad is close."

A rabbi across from her shifted in his seat. "I feel it too."

A third voice, quieter than the others, spoke from the far side of the circle.

"It is not going to be stopped," the man said, "but we must pray, or it could be worse."

The room fell still.

John felt the warning. His nerves rattled.

He bowed his head.

"Lord," he prayed, "protect the delegates, and our leaders, and may the plans of any evildoers be thwarted. And for President Tchi — *A thousand may fall at your side, and ten thousand at your right hand, but it shall not approach you* (Psalm 91:7). That said, Lord, may Your Will be done."

No one spoke after that.

The silence deepened.

Then a phone buzzed on the table.

And another.

One of the aides standing by the wall looked down at his screen, drained of color. He projected it as a hologram for John and all to see. A news alert. Before anyone explained, the video replay began to circulate.

On the hologram, President Tchi and Vice President Cheryl Agnewski were stepping from their vehicle near the stadium entrance. The footage was shaky at first, then steady.

There was a crack no one fully heard on the recording because screams and movement swallowed the sound. Agnewski had lurched, stepped across President Tchi's path without knowing why, and took the bullet. Tchi staggered a split second later, hit by the same shot or a second so close it may as well have been one.

Secret Service moved with terrifying speed, bodies closing, agents shoving, shouting, covering, dragging the President down and away while people scattered in every direction.

Vice President Agnewski died on impact.

President Tchi was rushed to Walter Reed.

The room where John sat remained eerily quiet.

No one had words for what they had just seen. They had hoped…

John stared at the replay and thought of the prayers. The anticipated assailant had not been stopped. But the outcome wasn't the worst it could have been either. A terrible mercy had intervened. The Vice President, without meaning to, had crossed into the path of death and preserved the President's life.

John closed his eyes.

"Rest her soul, Lord," he whispered. "And spare this nation more heartache. Please, not another war."

By midday, the summit was in danger of collapsing under the weight of the morning.

Every hallway swirled in blame, fear, rumor, suspicion. Delegates huddled by country. Security doubled. Faces that had arrived polished for cameras now looked raw and frazzled. No real work was getting done. The nation froze.

John asked the White House staff to seat everyone for the planned midday meal in the State Ballroom.

They listened.

That in itself was something.

When the room had settled enough for plates to be set and doors to close, John stepped to the microphone. The clatter of silverware faded. Interpreters leaned forward. Heads turned.

"This will not be a prayer only for the food," he said. "It needs to be more than that."

The room quieted further.

"May we quiet our minds, and release blame for today's unfortunate loss. We have a great deal to accomplish while we are together. You did not pull the trigger. No one here did. Let's focus and let go of any ideas we have to save the day, save our reputation, or change what's already been done.

"We will find who did this, and I'm confident justice will be swift. But until then, let us pray for the President of the United States and his family, and for the Vice President—rest in peace—and her family. May the power of God bring the President to full health as quickly as possible.

"I have a story to share, and I ask you to listen as lunch continues to be served."

The staff moved about diligently while John remained at the mic.

He told them the old Chinese farmer story.

There was once a farmer whose horse ran away. The neighbors came and said, "What BAD luck."

The farmer replied, "Maybe."

The next day the horse returned, bringing with it several wild horses. The neighbors said, "What GOOD luck."

The farmer replied, "Maybe."

The day after that, the farmer's son tried to ride one of the wild horses, was thrown, and broke his leg. The neighbors said, "What BAD luck."

The farmer replied, "Maybe."

Then war came, and soldiers arrived in the village to conscript every able-bodied young man. Because the son's leg was broken, they left him behind. The neighbors said, "What GOOD luck."

And once again, the farmer replied, "Maybe."

By the time John finished, the room had softened. He looked over the crowd of gathered leaders.

"So you see," he said, "we do not know yet whether today's events are to be judged as solely good or bad. We place our faith in God and rest assured that all events can be made good when we turn our attention to Him."

Something in the room shifted after that.

Not everyone leaned in spiritually, but enough did. Some saw the wisdom immediately. Others respected that the United States was taking the spiritual dimension seriously. A few simply seemed relieved to be invited into stillness instead of performance.

And one man, more than the others, watched John carefully through the whole thing.

President Han Zhiyu of China.

When John told the farmer story, Zhiyu's expression changed almost imperceptibly. It was his favorite fable. He had not expected to hear it in the White House, much less from a machinist-preacher from Kentucky holding together a summit on the day an American vice president had been killed.

Before the lunch ended, Zhiyu's aide approached discreetly and asked whether the President of China might have a private word with John during the afternoon breakout sessions.

John agreed.

They met in the Map Room.

It was small enough to feel private but official enough not to invite suspicion. A White House staffer closed the door behind them. Only one interpreter remained, but Zhiyu dismissed him after a few opening pleasantries.

"I would prefer English," Zhiyu said. "We can manage."

He studied John for a moment before speaking again.

"The story you told at lunch," he said. "The farmer."

"Yes."

"My mother loved that story. She used to tell it whenever something went badly in our family. She believed time revealed truth better than fear."

John nodded.

"It's a good story."

Zhiyu looked toward the window, then back.

"I want what you did for your President," he said. "Not religion. Not conversion. But whatever allowed him to change."

John sat with that for a moment.

"I can help you listen," he said. "But I can't do it for you."

Zhiyu gave the slightest smile.

"Yes. I believe that."

He was not a Christian. That much was obvious. John could feel it in the language Zhiyu avoided and the language he welcomed. So John adjusted.

Instead of saying Holy Spirit or Jesus first, he spoke of

surrender, truth, and the divine source beneath the noise of the self.

"There is a teacher deeper than fear," John said. "You may call it something different than I do. That's alright. But if you want to hear clearly, you must cancel your goals for a moment."

Zhiyu's face tightened.

"My goal is to live," he said dryly.

"Exactly," John replied. "And for the next few minutes, you must even let go of that."

That got his attention.

John guided him slowly.

"Close your eyes. Breathe. Release trying to fix your health. Release trying to survive. Release trying to get an answer that comforts you. Then ask for whatever truth may assist your health."

Zhiyu followed, though not without resistance.

Several minutes passed.

His brow furrowed. His jaw tightened. His breathing changed.

Then something opened.

He inhaled sharply and opened his eyes.

"I saw a man," he said.

John stayed quiet.

"A doctor. Chinese. I know his face, but I do not know him personally. He is in Chengdu." He swallowed. "He can help me."

"With what?" John asked.

Zhiyu looked away.

"With something I have not shared."

John nodded once. That was enough.

He did not need to know.

The room went still.

But then Zhiyu's face shifted. Shame moved through it, then anger.

"There is more," he said.

John waited.

Zhiyu looked sick with what he was seeing in his spirit.

"There is someone near me," he said. "Someone who would gain from chaos. Someone close enough to act under cover of loyalty."

He stood and paced once before regaining himself.

"I am ashamed," he said. "Ashamed that this could be true. Angry that I did not see it. Embarrassed that an American sees the rot in my house before I do."

John rose too, but kept distance. "Truth is mercy," he said. "Even when it wounds pride."

Zhiyu let out a bitter breath.

"If this becomes public too soon, it could trigger exactly what the assassin wanted. War. Retribution. Collapse."

John nodded. "I will not speak to the press."

"You may tell President Tchi," Zhiyu said. "No one else."

They left it there.

That was enough for one room, one hour, one day.

Within weeks, China confirmed through secure channels that men tied to the assassination had indeed been found and neutralized in a way that ensured they would never harm another.

President Zhiyu kept his word.

And because the private meeting in the Map Room had affected him deeply, he invited John to coach members of his own delegation in spiritual honesty and discernment. What began as damage control became an unlikely bridge between the two nations.

It was a fortuitous invitation.

John would need China more than he yet understood.

By June, President Tchi knew who he wanted to replace Vice President Agnewski.

John.

The decision did not come out of nowhere. In the months following the summit, the two men grew close in a way neither had expected. They prayed together, argued sometimes, laughed more than either would have guessed, and learned to trust each other.

John met with him often—sometimes in formal briefings, other times late at night over tea when pain from the wound kept Tchi from sleeping.

Steph occasionally joined them. She saw it—saw the way Tchi looked at John. Respect.

The President never fully recovered from being shot. He remained sharp. His spirit remained strong. But his body had changed.

Travel exhausted him. Long days hollowed him out. Recovery came slower than he had hoped, and the office did not permit weakness.

One month before the announcement, John told Steph what God had already revealed in prayer.

"I'm going to be asked," he said.

"To be Vice President?" She finished.

He nodded.

"And?"

"God said to be ready and to accept. He also said He'd raise up a council around me so His plans could succeed."

Steph smiled like someone hearing what she already suspected.

"Then when he asks you," she embraced him and whispered, "say yes."

She didn't flinch at the prospect of her husband being a heartbeat away from the Presidency. Not once.

The ask came in a quiet private moment.

No cameras. No aides. No ceremony.

Just Tchi, tired and worn at the edges, seated in a private room off the residence with a blanket over his legs.

"John," he said, "I need you to be my Vice President."

John nodded and said, "Yes, sir. God's been preparing me. I will serve Him first, you know."

Tchi's eyes softened. "I knew you'd say that."

John smiled faintly. "This will be a good thing."

"Yes," Tchi said. "It will."

The announcement rattled the country.

Some applauded the choice. Others mocked it. Critics called it reckless; supporters called it inspired.

John was painted in some circles as a holy fraud, a Kentucky manipulator, a snake-oil mystic who had somehow hypnotized a wounded President.

More extreme voices claimed he had colluded with China, orchestrated events, or used spirituality as cover for a quiet coup.

None of it was true.

But truth couldn't slow the noise.

Security around John's family increased. Secret Service details expanded to include his children, grandchildren, and extended movements. Agents escorting his grandkids to school became strangely normal.

Vice President John Smith learned quickly that power did not simplify life. It magnified everything.

Still, he remained steady.

A year passed in the vice presidency.

John grew into the role not by loving politics, but by refusing to let politics define the work. He prayed with generals, quieted cabinet secretaries, met privately with ambassadors, and increasingly became the place President Tchi went when the outer landscape grew too noisy to read clearly.

But the President's body continued to fail him.

One day John was summoned to the Oval Office and told to bring his family.

He arrived with Steph, Sarah, and the others expecting bad news, though not this.

Tchi looked exhausted. Not merely tired—spent. The shooting had taken more from him than he had admitted publicly, and the office had asked more of him than his body could now give.

He stood when they entered, balanced by a cane.

"Sit," he said gently. "All of you. Please."

John knew this was a big deal.

Tchi looked at him first.

Then at Steph.

Then at the family.

"I'm stepping down," he said flatly.

No one spoke.

"It is for the good of the country," he continued. "I hoped my strength would return more fully. It has not. The pace is no longer wise. There will be another election in 2036, and I want the people to have a fair chance to choose. But I also want the nation protected until then."

He looked directly at John.

"God needs you, John. The nation needs you. And I need you."

It hit harder than John expected.

This was no longer an office changing hands. This was his friend surrendering something he had fought dearly to hold.

John swallowed.

"I never wanted this seat," he said honestly.

"I know," Tchi replied. "That's one of the reasons you must have it."

Tears stood in Steph's eyes. Sarah reached for her mother's hand.

John bowed his head.

"If this is the will of God," he said quietly, "I will take it."

What followed became one of the strangest constitutional seasons in American history.

Congress, moved by the assassination attempt, the President's condition, and the need for continuity, passed emergency measures allowing Tchi to step down. In an unprecedented arrangement, he accepted the Vice Presidency under the man he had himself named to it. The two men found the arrangement easier than the country did. Critics called it an unlawful improvisation. Supporters called it necessary compassion. Legal scholars argued for weeks. Social media devoured it all.

But the transfer happened.

And on October 13, 2035, by divine providence and extraordinary national circumstance, John Smith—machinist, preacher, counselor of the soul—became President of the United States.

The country erupted.

Some celebrated continuity. Others cried constitutional crisis. Though many on both sides called him America's healer, pundits fought nightly over whether he was a stabilizing force, a religious threat, or a dangerous idealist elevated beyond his station.

Behind closed doors, only a select few knew how delicate the truth really was.

John and Tchi knew China had played a deeper role in the assassination attempt than the public would ever be allowed to hear. They also knew how quickly that truth could ignite not justice, but catastrophe—war, retaliation, pride, the old cycle rising again.

John did not want revenge.

He wanted peace.

China would be his path toward freedom, not because he trusted them, but because he trusted God enough to walk where fear said not to go.

Like the knight in a story he once heard about overcoming fear, John knew he had to enter the dragon's mouth to defeat the dragon.

Into the mouth of the dragon—his enemy—he would climb.

CHAPTER 12
CHINA

"Unless a grain of wheat falls into the earth and dies, it remains alone; but if it dies, it bears much fruit.
— John 12:24

One of John's first actions as President was to visit China. The night before departure, Jesus visited.

"John."

He sat up in bed. The room was dim. The clock read 10:00 PM. Steph slept peacefully beside him, undisturbed. The White House had become their temporary quarters, borrowed space that still didn't feel like a home.

"Open your Bible to Revelation," Jesus said.

John felt physically worn from the day, but his spirit reached for the Bible without hesitation. He flipped through the familiar pages, and as he turned to the final book, something shifted. The words didn't sit still. They seemed alive—lifting, dancing, opening.

"Trust me," Jesus said. "You need to see this before your trip. Don't worry about sleep. You will be rested."

John nodded. "I trust you."

The room faded.

He was no longer reading.

He was there.

"I'm with him," John said quietly. "On the island… Patmos."

Wind moved across the rocks. The sea pressed against the shore in steady rhythm. He saw John the Apostle, weathered, steady, writing.

"And you're there," John continued. "You're appearing to him… radiant. He's immersed. Listening."

Jesus did not interrupt. He simply witnessed John's awe.

"I see a map with seven cities. The letters…" John said. "You're speaking and he's writing… to the churches."

John moved closer—no longer observing, but sharing the space.

"This one is to Ephesus. Looks like a port city where modern day Turkey sits," he said. "They've worked hard. Tested false teachers to protect the truth. But they've lost the warmth and passion they had for God and each other. You call them back to remember how it felt in the early days... to love like they did before."

John looked up from the letter, amazed that he was witnessing this in real-time—present with St. John and Jesus. He smiled, feeling great love, before returning his attention to the second letter.

"This one is to Smyrna, another port city just north of the first letter's city of Ephesus... they've remained faithful despite suffering and mistreatment suppressing them in the pagan city. Nonetheless, they are rich in spirit. You're telling them not to be afraid—stay strong even if they suffer or die. You will give them the crown of life."

He breathed in slowly, getting mental glimpses of the cities as he read.

"Pergamum is next—north of Smyrna on a mountaintop. St. John's frowning and shaking his head. Some remain loyal to you despite being surrounded by evil. Others drift into idol worship and sin. '*Stop listening to those lies. Turn back to Me.*' You say."

The scenes unfolded like movie clips. Each church revealed a pattern in them and in humanity.

"Thyatira is loving, faithful and growing in good works. However, a false teacher has led people astray. You tell them to hold on to the truth, that you will reward those who stay faithful and refuse evil. You promise authority over the nations to those who keep your ways until the end."

John felt the weight of that consequence. The rewards of faith and surrender... real.

The next two letters had similar themes. In Sardis, most pretended to follow God, but their hearts were asleep. The Laodiceans were lukewarm. Thought they didn't need God. They were wrong. "You say: *Come back to Me. I'm knocking on the door of your heart — open it and let Me in.*"

John felt this was for him too. He said quietly, "Yes, Lord. I open my heart to you."

"And the last one is Philadelphia..." he said softly. "They

hold on and endure. You've opened a door for them no one can shut. You promise their reward is coming soon."

Jesus' presence remained steady beside him on the island.

"Do you see it?" Jesus asked gently.

John nodded. "That the letters… they're not just for them?"

"Correct." Jesus confirmed. "They're for all of you."

The vision changed as a door to heaven opened for St. John.

A voice spoke, "Come up here and I will show you what must happen afterwards."

St. John rose into heaven—John pulled along with him.

"I see the throne," John said. "God's sitting holding a sealed scroll, surrounded by angels singing. Light fills everything. Living color."

"You, Jesus… You're the one who opens the scroll," John said. "The perfect Lamb. God's plan for the world… it moves through you."

He witnessed Jesus opening seals on the scroll. Mesmerized. Present.

Each seal revealed what would unfold when we turned from God.

"I see conquerors, wars, famine, death, martyrs, earthquakes and storms. It's awful! And it's not random… is it?" John asked.

"No more than a splash is random when you jump in water," Jesus remarked.

"I see. These are the consequences of choices." John's emotions rose. Eyes watered. His compassion for the suffering mixed with awareness of his own failures.

"Forgive me, Lord." The tears fell. He paused to breathe and center, feeling Jesus' embrace.

"Keep watching," Jesus said.

The chaos continued, but something else was present.

"It's not as bad as it could be." John said, quieter now. "Mercy is there. Four angels are holding back the suffering.

They're saying: *Not yet. Do not harm the earth, or the sea, or the trees—not until those belonging to God are sealed… those who have surrendered their way to live as one with Christ, one with God."*

"You did that." John said. You opened the way for our salvation. I think I get it."

"Yes, John. I am the way. And it is through transformation—becoming what I am—that they come to the Father. We plan to unify all into God's Kingdom. The path is here. Keep watching. There's more."

John stayed with the images, "I see sealed tribes of Israel. Time passes. Generations rise and fall. And now, today. Their descendants live. What is this?"

"John, you live in the end times. You have a part to play. All are invited, but a relationship is optional. You said 'yes' and I am happy you did. Thank you. More and more are choosing. The path is clear. "

Jesus turned to open the seventh seal.

John narrated, "There are seven angels blowing trumpets. Each one brings a disaster. A great shaking to awaken the people —more chances to turn to God.

"Fires, earthquakes and large volcanoes erupt. The waters turn undrinkable. Many die. Then darkness filled the skies. An eagle flies warning of the next three trumpets: A painful insect invasion followed by one-third of the population dying horribly. Then, before the tenth and final trumpet, St. John eats the scroll." John relayed.

"Just as Ezekiel had before him." Jesus emphasized.

John looked confused, then startled.

"The last trumpet sounded. God's kingdom is being announced: *The kingdom of the world has become the kingdom of our Lord and of His Christ; and He will reign forever and ever' (Revelation 11:15).*

"Christ is the King, rightfully restored with the Father." John said, realizing Jesus invited him into that very union. "I see the nations enraged. Their plans to undermine you failed. Your wrath is unleashed. The dead are judged. You reward those loyal to you. It's the glory of the Lord. I see it all." John said.

Jesus added, "All are invited."

That reassured John. There was still time.

"These aren't punishments." John said. "You're calling us. Trying to wake us up."

"Yes. Look." Jesus said pointing to a woman in pain.

"I see her," John said. "About to give birth."

Jesus explained, "She's the nurturing side of the soul: Wisdom, intuition, and love giving birth to new consciousness… new awareness.

John hadn't fully understood Revelation before. Context helps. "There's a dragon. What does that mean?"

Jesus answered, "It's the old fear-based nature trying to stop the birth. But John, the child, the Christ within, is protected. Unstoppable. And will rise to union with God."

John's eyes flickered under their lids, fully invested in the vision. The scenes came faster.

"The beast… the need to control. The voice that justifies it… the false prophet."

John paused.

"It's not just out there," he said. "It's in us."

Jesus let that revelation settle in John.

"And Babylon…" John continued. "The whole false structure. Built on image, power, possession… it looks strong until it collapses.

The collapse then, isn't destruction. It's release… a dismantling of everything we built to *achieve* God.

"And all this leads to..." John said softer, "union. The wedding feast. No separation left. God… and man… no longer divided."

The final images of the vision unfolded.

"The dragon has returned," John said. "One last attempt. Then—gone from the world."

"I thought the world would be destroyed," John said. "But instead, it appears healed and transformed."

"Yes," Jesus said. "Stripped of the curse of sin—perfected. You see the light that remains?"

"Yes," John answered. "There it is. A new Jerusalem," he whispered. "Descending from heaven. Here. In us. In the world."

He exhaled.

"That's Revelation, isn't it?"

Silence.

Then Jesus spoke again.

"John… it's time."

Rather than fading, the vision deepened.

"Do you see why you must remember who you are?"

John nodded.

"I do."

"You are part of this," Jesus said. "I am in you. You are in the Father. We are one. This is the revelation."

The scene changed again.

He was no longer above Patmos. No longer witnessing St. John in heaven.

He, himself, was before the throne where St. John had stood, knelt.

Color beyond color. Light beyond light. A presence of immense love filled everything—welcoming him.

From within the brilliance, he saw Jesus' face emerge from the heart of God. One source. One light. Two *bodies*.

John fell to his knees in reverence.

"Rise, my son," came the voice as a strong thought. "Be not afraid."

John stood.

"You will come home to me soon."

He understood and felt joy. He could have stayed forever had it been God's plan. He was caught up in the moment.

"This is not yours to carry alone," the voice continued.

"There are many more. You are part of what is unfolding. Go to China. Accept what comes."

And then—he was back.

The room.

The bed.

Steph asleep beside him.

The clock read 4:00 AM.

It was time to go.

The flight to China was quiet.

God spoke in his heart. John was to accept the outcome of the meeting even if it didn't match his expectations. He sensed disappointment coming.

"I release control." He whispered to himself as he looked over his goals:

- China embraces U.S. as ally
- Free and fair trade
- Release U.S. from sanctions
- Reduced surveillance
- Remove control grid dependencies

The U.S. lost many freedoms following their glory days. John wanted grace from their recent enemy. What he wanted didn't matter. Only obedience to God did.

When they landed, Beijing was covered in a low mist. It clung to the ground and softened the lights of the city. It was just past 11:30 PM.

A small delegation greeted them.

John's team was intentionally light—just four of them plus secret service. This was not a show, but a delicate conversation to shape the future… hopefully.

At the guesthouse, the four gathered in the kitchen.

Snacks on the counter. Lights dimmed.

A device set at the center of the island created a cone of silence.

There could be no leaks. No recordings.

Just truth.

Jane Alcousta, Secretary of State, spoke first.

"Sir, we must expect deception. There's no version of this where they hand us back freedoms we once had. We lost the war. That has consequences. The smartest move is to listen, stabilize, and build toward something long-term. Short-term... we're cooked. We're not in control here. We should get in line with their agenda, and plan behind the scenes for an opportunity to fight when the time is right."

John nodded. "Thank you, Jane."

He let the words sit.

"But relax. Slow it down."

That got her attention.

"Over time," he said, "patterns play out. Cycles of behavior. Every civilization. Every era. We can interrupt them... or repeat them. We're in a pattern."

He looked at her.

"You see it, don't you?"

Jane stepped forward slightly.

"I think so. The world becomes distracted," she said. "Material things. Control. Power. Truth gets buried. Convenience replaces conscience. Spiritual emptiness guts institutions. Of course, truth-tellers see it all and call attention to it, but are silenced. People wake up to the crisis in stages as the system collapses. After collapse they return to what matters—faith, humility, love, connection. And then it starts again. They are like seasons: Spring. Summer. Fall. Winter. We're in spring. The old way is dead. The new is rebirthing."

John nodded.

"Yes... and."

Sarah leaned in. "And?" she asked.

John glanced at her.

She stood beside him—both as a daughter and someone who'd earned her place.

At twenty, her presence still surprised people who didn't know her.

Those who did didn't question it.

After the accident, and coma, something in Sarah had transformed. The world lost its grip on her. Something deeper took hold.

President Tchi saw it as she occasionally joined John at the White House—no longer to watch movies, but to learn.

When an internship with the National Security Advisor opened, she took it. She entered the White House quietly as an intern, observing, developing. She saw things others missed. Only nineteen at the time, she respected protocol and rarely spoke in meetings. Never interrupted.

Because of this, when she did interrupt for the first time, it stopped the room cold.

"No."

That was all she said.

The Secretary of State had snapped at her.

President Tchi had intervened.

"Let her speak."

"It's not right," she had said. "The intelligence. Something's missing."

She couldn't explain it.

But she was right.

And after that, when Sarah spoke, people listened. Within a month of saying 'No', she left school to work full-time.

Now she observed John.

"What's the 'and'?" she asked.

John turned back to the group.

"You're describing the outer pattern," he said. "But the outer follows from the inner."

Gerald, John's most trusted economic advisor, crossed his arms. "You're saying this is psychological?"

"I'm saying it's spiritual, psychological, biological," John replied. "And practical."

He scanned their faces. The *lights* hadn't come on yet.

"We saw it during the mental health pandemic with Marcus[3] and the others who broke free," he continued. "Remember? Change your inner world, the outer responds. Interestingly enough, it's also what John shared in the Book of Revelation."

Gerald exhaled. "You're not about to tell us we're living in Revelation, John."

John smiled and nodded.

"We are."

A pause.

"No," Gerald said. "Didn't we just go through Armageddon?"

"Exactly," John said, his tone steady, but engaged. "The cycles of Revelation, seen through the lens of history, have repeated again and again. The only part we seem to miss… is the return of Christ."

He let that sit a moment.

"But what if we've been looking at that wrong? Or at least… incompletely?"

Jane crossed her arms slightly and pursed her lips. "Go on."

John reached into the refrigerator, pulled out water bottles, and handed them around—giving the room a moment to settle.

"I met a woman once—Colette. She came through my church back in Kentucky. At the time, I didn't fully understand what she was saying. But it's making sense now."

He leaned lightly against the counter.

"What if the way we're looking for Christ's return is the same way many looked for the Messiah before Jesus came?"

That caught them.

"They expected a warrior," John continued. "Someone to overthrow Rome. Restore power. Fix the world externally."

He paused.

"That's not what they got."

The room stayed quiet.

"And most of them missed Him because of it." Gerald concluded

Jane's posture softened slightly. She uncrossed her arms.

"So you're saying..." she began, "...we might be doing the same thing now?"

John nodded.

"If we take Revelation only literally, then yes—we can expect chaos, destruction, something dramatic from the outside."

He looked at each of them. The *lights* were coming on.

"But if we also see it symbolically... and internalize it... then we start to see things as they are, not just as we've been taught to expect them."

Jane relaxed further. "Alright," she said. "I'll bite."

She leaned forward slightly.

"What's your theory?"

"Revelation isn't just events," he said. "It's a process of transformation. Inside a person. Inside a community. Inside a world."

No one moved. All eyes on John.

"Until we collectively transform, we're destined to repeat our outer patterns. So my theory? We change history by changing ourselves."

"How so?" Sarah asked. "We can't just push religion on everyone."

"No, but we have an opportunity with China to bring about a change for their best interests."

"Yeah right, dad, I mean John. Their best interests are for their control grid to manipulate the west... the world."

"I know, but God can make good of anything. There has to be a way to plant seeds of transformation inside their grid. China has their agenda. Let's help them get what they want, and open a gateway to share truth, wisdom, and a roadmap for transformation that anyone can access?"

"This is sounding interesting now." Gerald said.

Heads nodded.

"Last night… I didn't sleep much." John said. "Jesus shared insights about the Book of Revelation. It was like I was there. I know that sounds strange, but indulge me for a minute."

They were used to John and his divine stories. He waved for the group to follow him from the kitchen to a more comfortable seating area.

Sarah took her shoes off. Jane followed suit. The fireplace lights danced past the circle of chairs. John sat forward placing the cone of silence on a stained glass coffee table.

They settled. John continued.

"Let's look at the Book of Revelation from a different perspective.

"The throne," he said, "is the place of God within, already seated in every heart. The Lamb… is Christ joining our awareness. When that happens, everything changes. Mercy transforms judgment. Decisions flow from love instead of fear."

Their eyes were bright. Tracking.

"Then the seals open to the hidden layers of a person's heart."

He tapped his chest lightly.

"Pride. Fear. Desire. Control. Apathy. Denial. All of it exposed."

Gerald nodded slowly. "The horsemen…"

"Exactly," John said. "Not just out there. In here. They collapse the ego's defenses. Old patterns of conquest, anger, hunger for validation, and hopelessness—the white, red, black and pale horses—dissolve. "

"That would be quite a loss for people." Jane said. "They'll lose their minds."

"Not necessarily." Sarah piped in. "With proper training they'll realize what feels like loss is actually purification — preparing their soul for God's return."

"That's right , Sarah."

The conversation deepened.

Questions came.

Pushback.

Clarification.

They didn't just listen—they engaged.

"The beast?" Jane asked.

"Part of the ego," John said. "Demanding worship, importance, and control. "

"And the false prophet?"

"The voice that justifies it. Confirming *'You're right, you need this, and you deserve more.'*"

Sarah's open mouth closed.

"Wow! It's all right there."

Gerald frowned slightly as he sat forward. "Alright… but what about the mark of the beast?"

Jane nodded. "Yeah. That's always been tied to systems. Control. Buying and selling. That's not just… internal."

John didn't answer immediately—connecting to wisdom deeper than knowledge.

"It shows up in systems," he said finally. "But it doesn't start there."

Sarah tilted her head. "So where does it start?"

John tapped lightly against his chest again.

"Here."

A pause.

"The mark isn't something placed on a person," he continued. "It can be, but that would, again, be an outer manifestation of something that started within. The mark of the beast is something agreed to."

Jane crossed her arms again. "Agreed to how?"

"When a person decides—consciously or not—that they must secure their life apart from God."

Gerald stretched his neck. "Meaning?"

"Meaning," John said, "when survival becomes more important than truth… when control feels safer than trust…

when identity comes from what we have instead of who we are."

He looked at each of them.

"That's the agreement."

The room was quiet.

"And once enough people make that agreement," John continued, "the world starts to organize around it."

Jane's expression shifted. "So the system…"

She paused.

"…is the reflection," John finished.

Sarah's eyes lit up. "That's why it's tied to buying and selling."

John nodded.

"Money becomes the easiest way to measure worth, control access, and enforce participation. Not because money is evil—but because fear knows how to use it."

Gerald exhaled slowly. "So you're saying the 'beast system' isn't created first…"

"It emerges," John said. "From unresolved fear."

Jane shook her head slightly, thinking it through. "And the forehead… the hand…"

"They represent thoughts and actions," Sarah said quietly.

John smiled at her.

"Exactly."

Another pause settled over the room.

"So what does it mean to *not* take the mark?" Gerald asked.

John's tone softened.

"It means you no longer let fear decide who you are."

Silence.

"You can still live in the system," he continued. "Use money. Work. Build. But you're not owned by it. You're not defined by it. You're not of the world any more than Jesus was" (John 17:14).

Jane let out a quiet breath. "So the battle isn't out there at all."

John shook his head gently.

"It never was."

The room fell silent for several minutes.

Then Gerald asked, "What about Babylon?"

"The false self," John said. "Everything built on image instead of truth. Possessions. Recognition. Pleasure. Feels grand until it collapses."

"When inner Babylon falls, people will feel so lost." Jane said.

"I've been there," John looked toward the window. "I felt the emptiness, the confusion. But it's not something to fear. It's liberation! Freedom from the false self. End of the illusion."

"And what's left?" Jane asked.

John's expression brightened.

"God."

Silence. Then:

"And at the end… the end of days?" Gerald asked.

John looked at him. "It's not the end."

He paused. "It's union."

He let that sit.

"No more separation," he said. "That's the point of all of it."

The room was lighter. They were not yet convinced of everything, but space had been created for something.

They were open. Awake.

John glanced at the clock.

"We'll talk specifics in the morning," he said. "Get some rest."

They nodded.

Slowly, they dispersed.

John remained a moment longer. The city lights filtered through the mist outside.

China. The dragon—beyond a symbol, but a place.

Any remaining fear had transformed. Repurposed by love.

His phone buzzed once on the stained glass table.

Steph.

> Psalm 91. All of it. I love you.

He read it twice. Smiled. Tapped back.

> I love you. See you soon.

Set the phone face-down on the table.

He knew what was ahead. Not the details, but the foreboding. The anticipation, meaning, and cost.

The next day would be the most important day of his life.

He sensed it could be his last.

Yet still, he went.

CHAPTER 13
HEALING WORLDS

"And other sheep I have, which are not of this fold: them also I must bring."
— John 10:16

President Han Zhiyu, leader of China, stood before the Great Hall of the People on the western edge of Tiananmen Square, where a crisp wind carried the echo of drums across the vast plaza. John and his team approached along the red carpet, flanked by the Honor Guard of the People's Liberation Army.

They shook hands and stood side by side as flags lifted. National anthems of both countries were performed by military bands.

Then silence returned.

Another handshake and photo.

They turned toward the marble steps and entered.

Inside, they were led into the East Hall. The press remained outside, waiting for whatever outcome would shape the next chapter of the world.

If all went well, there would be a celebratory banquet inside the Great Hall.

If not—

no one said it.

They sat across from one another.

Measured. Still.

Watching.

China had plans for the United States—conditions of surrender. They would rewrite its constitution, dismantle its military, and restructure its economy and political system.

The United States had done the same to Japan after World War II. It was called reconstruction—partnership. And over time, sovereignty returned, but always within a system shaped by American power.

Now the roles had reversed.

The language was different.

The structure was not.

John wasn't there to argue history.

He was there to interrupt it.

China's surveillance was too much.

"President Zhiyu," John began, "I want to share a story with you."

Zhiyu nodded once.

"Go on."

John leaned forward slightly.

"A nuclear bomb was detonated in Detroit near the end of the war. All signs pointed to China. Our generals pressed for retaliation. The public demanded it."

He paused.

"We had the capability—assets in the region. The systems to respond were active. The authority was clear."

Zhiyu's eyes narrowed slightly.

"And yet… you did not respond."

"No," John said. "We chose restraint."

"Why?"

"Tchi was actually Vice President at the time. He had a hunch," John said. "Who would have benefited had we struck you?"

Zhiyu didn't answer.

"Russia," John continued. "They wanted us to retaliate and for China to further crush the U.S. in return. Incinerate us."

"Why do you think that was?" Zhiyu asked.

"Russia blamed us for a lab leak in Ukraine. Believed it fueled the global mental health pandemic."

Zhiyu nodded, believing this to be true. "Those nutrient blockers led to pyrrole disorders—mass mania."

"Yes," John replied. "Thankfully, that crisis has been

resolved. As you know, Russia called for war crimes trials against U.S. leaders. They didn't get support for those trials—expected China to have their backs. But you pulled away."

"We had bigger fish to fry, as you say in the U.S." Zhiyu said.

"Yes. Yes. Bigger fish to fry." John repeated realizing the entire U.S. was the bigger fish.

John continued. "As it turned out, Russian sleeper cells found refuge in the mountains of Montana where they assembled tiny nuclear explosives. When Russia felt isolated, they attacked using Chinese double agents."

A quiet understanding passed between them.

"President Tchi chose restraint. Wise choice," Zhiyu said. "Why tell me this now?"

John held his gaze.

"Because we have a chance to end this pattern of hostility."

The room remained still.

"There is something beneath war and peace," John said. "A pattern that repeats until its roots dissolve."

He spoke plainly, though drew from scripture.

"The pattern goes back to the beginning of time, to the source of life that only knows love. We were made from it… and for it. But we choose to separate from it."

He gestured lightly.

"And when we do, we search for its replacement from the world. We search for meaning. For identity. For control."

Zhiyu patiently listened.

"We build systems to replace what we've lost. Systems for power, possessions, pleasures, and structure."

He paused.

"But none of it satisfies. At some point we realize our mistake and seek a return. The return is a kind death—an awakening, a purification, a transformation that births something new in a person. One goes through temptation, collapse, cleansing. We call it the living Christ—a restored union with Source, God. Completion."

Zhiyu watched him closely.

"You are describing the Taoist return," he said.

John nodded. "Then help me understand it as you see it."

Zhiyu spoke—not as a politician now, but as someone who had walked a path.

"In Taoist thought, awakening begins by seeing through the illusion and knowing oneself. As Laozi wrote, when you know yourself, wisdom opens.

From there comes the cultivation of the Way—a refining of the heart through stillness, breath, and right living.

As the noise settles, something deeper begins to emerge—the true self that was always there.

Then comes the testing. The old patterns rise again—pride, lust, fear, the pull for control. The temptation reveals what still holds you.

If you stay, if you don't turn away,

there is a collapse of the person you thought you were.

The false center gives way,

and what remains is clarity and stillness.

The heart becomes like clear water, its purification complete.

In that stillness, separation fades. There is union with the Tao where the individual and Source are no longer two.

And then, you return to society, no longer seeking, but embodying the Tao through ordinary life—in words, in work, in presence. This is the completion. Embodiment."

He looked at John.

"You call it living as Christ and a New Jerusalem."

John didn't hide his surprise.

"You've studied."

"I've lived," Zhiyu replied.

He paused. Then:

"What are you proposing?"

John dove right in. "I'd like the freedom to have our nation live by these principles. In order to do that we have to teach it. Your system locks us down—prevents what we just discussed.

I don't just want people to know about Jesus, but be transformed by Him... To live as He taught. To become what He showed is possible."

He let that sink in before continuing.

"I'm not asking for control. I'm asking for space. Because this doesn't work by force. It never has."

He steadied his gaze on Zhiyu.

"What I've been learning... what we've been talking about... it's not just for me. And it's not just for my country.

God has already placed this path everywhere. Across traditions. Across nations. Different language... same invitation."

He leaned forward slightly.

"But it only works if people are free to step into it."

A pause.

"If we lead this way, by inviting transformation, rather than enforcing behavior, people begin to change from the inside out.

And when that happens,

you don't have to control them.

They become aligned and live harmoniously."

His voice softened, but didn't lose its edge.

"I want to see our nation reflect what Jesus prayed for in John 17—for all to live as one with God—a people living in Christ. Not in theory. Not later. Soon. I believe the next second coming of Christ could include everyone. I believe this world can become heaven on earth."

A breath.

"But it requires something."

He held Zhiyu's gaze. Lowered his finger from pointing at the ceiling and touched his heart.

"People have to lay down the life they think they're protecting... and be willing to be re-born into this new life. That's where it begins.

We can do this as leaders inviting transformation rather than governments enforcing behavior. If we do, we break the cycle."

Silence.

Zhiyu sat back.

"We are not ready for this, John," he said with certainty.

"People will not choose this," Zhiyu continued. "You've seen the inner turmoil of our nations playing out: Dysfunction. Disorder. War."

His tone sharpened with conviction.

"They must be guided. Structured. Corrected. Forced if necessary. We've tried letting people choose. It doesn't work. Incentives are needed.

John, you and I know better. We must not wait any longer. You are a good man, but idealistic in your nature. You think people will choose and I know they will not."

Suddenly, John saw it. An image formed in his mind. Lucifer stood opposed to Jesus—not in equal authority, but in opposition of methods.

One sought to force what could only be given. To bend, pressure, and remove choice until surrender was inevitable.

The other did not argue. He lived it. He showed it. He invited.

John felt the difference more than he understood it.

Control… or love. Compulsion… or freedom.

The image shifted. Lucifer fell, unable to remain in what he refused to become.

And the pattern continued. Across time. Across nations. Empires rising on control… falling under their own weight.

Now he saw it again.

The United States… fading.

China… rising.

Another expression of the same ancient pull. Force shaping the world from the outside.

Zhiyu leaned forward slightly.

"There is another way," he said.

John said nothing.

"We implement the system," Zhiyu continued. "Structure. Surveillance. Stability."

A pause.

"But we give you space inside it."

John's eyes didn't move.

"You teach your transformation," Zhiyu said. "Carefully. Gradually. You shape the people—within the framework."

He studied him.

"You remain President. You lead. And over time… perhaps your vision comes to pass."

The room held its breath. John recognized Zhiyu offering what he thought he wanted. But it was different.

He didn't deliberate.

"That's not what I'm proposing," John said quietly.

Zhiyu's expression tightened.

"You want to shape behavior and call it transformation," John continued. "I'm talking about changing the heart… and letting behavior follow."

A tingling in his head caused him to pause longer than normal. The room leaned in. He closed with

"If it's forced… it isn't from love. Isn't from Source."

Something shifted in Zhiyu.

He had seen what happened when people were left to choose.

Chaos.

Collapse.

Loss.

His father's voice echoed somewhere deep within him:

Order must be protected. And yet—something in John's words carried strength. It felt… true.

Before he could respond, the room changed.

The atmosphere grew still. The temperature cooled.

John's eyes lifted.

Not to Zhiyu or to anyone.

"It's time," He said softly.

Sarah felt it too.

A stillness deeper than silence.

She turned, and saw.

Zhiyu saw it too, though he did not understand what he was seeing.

It was Jesus. He stood before them. Not in their minds, but present. Physical.

And at that moment, the question was no longer philosophical.

It was right in front of them.

"Be not afraid, my friends," He said, "I see you are at a threshold."

His voice calmed every nerve.

"You have reached the ripe time when civilizations can remember Christ eternal," Jesus continued. "And live in harmony as one."

He looked at John and said, "It is time."

A rush of air rose up from the floor as if a doorway above had opened. Time stood still.

"We will watch from afar," He said gently. "But you are being called home."

Jesus extended His hand.

John looked at it knowingly. Not what would happen, but that his *race* was over. And that was enough.

He took Jesus' hand.

For a moment… nothing happened.

Then—a gentle shimmer of light rose up.

John's body gave way.

It was gentle.

He surrendered his soul to Jesus… to heaven.

"Dad—"

Sarah was already moving.

But she knew.

Jane reached him next, her hand finding his shoulder.

"John…"

But there was no response.

Gerald turned away, one hand covering his mouth distressed.

No one spoke. Zhiyu remained standing, processing the situation. He had seen the impossible. Nothing he could prove. And yet… everything had changed.

His ideas of control had always made sense.

But the conversation. The timing. John's final words. For the first time in his life certainty was lost.

Zhiyu turned slowly toward the door. Then stopped.

"We will come to Washington," he said quietly to Gerald and paused. "There is more… to discuss."

He walked out.

Emergency personnel arrived within minutes. Sarah wept in Jane's arms. Gerald called Vice-President Tchi to relay events.

And nothing in the world was quite the same.

CHAPTER 14
RIGHT ACTION

"Be not conformed to this world: but be ye transformed by the renewing of your mind."
— Romans 12:2

As PROMISED, President Zhiyu flew to Washington after John's passing. Something unsettled in him.

He had spent a lifetime refining systems rooted in structure, control, precision. They reflected beliefs that if people were guided correctly, shaped carefully, the world could be made stable... even good.

And yet, in a single moment, something had occurred that no system could explain.

Seeing Jesus changed things for him. It was his first experience like that from the spiritual realm.

He questioned. Tried to deny what his eyes clearly saw. Wrestled with his beliefs. He journaled and discovered confusion, then clarity, and confusion again.

A pull on his heart to reconsider his positions felt compelling. But he didn't trust those feelings. He couldn't dismiss them either.

His last journal entry upon landing read, "Control or Invite?"

He and President Tchi soon were alone in the Oval Office. They casually met alone. The press kept in the dark just a little while longer.

"To John," Zhiyu said, raising a whiskey glass high above his head. Eyes on the heavens.

"To John," Tchi said. Neither drank the whiskey but both touched it to their lips.

They talked about John and agreed to honor him as a hero in the press. Honesty would win the day. Then the tone changed.

"I need your perspective," Zhiyu said and then explained his dilemma of Control or Invitation.

Tchi thoughtfully considered how to respond. Then the words came.

"Like you, I've never experienced the wisdom of God like I

did with John," Tchi replied. "If he believed people must choose… then I believe we should let them choose. At least in the U.S. You might continue your way in China, but let us do it our way here. Invite is the answer."

Zhiyu stood and walked near the window, thinking of his country that had learned to obey.

"If we're wrong," Zhiyu said, "we risk everything."

Tchi didn't respond right away.

"President Zhiyu. I want to take the risk. I trust our God and God is what people need. It's a risk worth taking."

That night, Zhiyu made a decision. He felt his nerves—the kind that arrive just before doing the right thing, just before shedding the past.

"I want to try John's way," he said the next morning over breakfast. "We will teach the path. Not enforce it."

He paused.

"Let people find their way back… in the language God gives them."

It felt foreign in his mouth. Uncomfortable. Unstructured. Uncontrolled. But he also felt free—unburdened and hopeful.

Later that day, he made a request.

"I'd like to meet with Sarah."

She arrived that evening covering grief with a smile. Memories of their previous meeting flooded her senses.

"Forgive me, Mr. President." She looked away, blotting the corners of her eyes with a tissue."

He understood. Jesus. The passing of her father. The tension. He understood.

Zhiyu studied her quietly. There was no ambition in her. No reaching like so many others.

Only a kind of stillness. He had seen it once before in John.

"I'd like you to be President of the United States," he said. Tchi had briefed her, but not for this.

Sarah blinked. Chuckled. But then she felt his seriousness and composed herself.

"It doesn't work that way," she said. "We have elections. And I'm only twenty."

Zhiyu didn't move.

"We'll prepare you. Perhaps in a few years. There are ways to make it happen. I think Tchi would even support you."

She shook her head.

"I wouldn't know how to be President. I'm not supposed to be President. I'm not my father."

Neither spoke. She had studied under John and was very interested in his mission. She'd do anything.

"I'll continue serving. Let me serve," she said. "That I understand."

Sarah walked the long hallway back to the residence. The lamps were dimmed.

Steph was at the kitchen table, John's phone face-up beside her tea. She had been reading something—reading it for a long time.

Sarah sat down across from her. Said nothing.

After a moment, Steph slid the phone across the table.

Sarah read what was on the screen.

Psalm 91. All of it. I love you.

> I love you. See you soon.

She closed her eyes.

"He answered," Steph whispered. "See you soon. Soon…"

"Mom—" Sarah's hand closed over her mom's.

"Do you think he knew?" Steph asked.

Sarah blinked and smiled. "I've wondered the same thing."

They sat with it.

Then Steph took a breath and looked up.

"What did Zhiyu want?"

Sarah hesitated.

"He offered me the Presidency."

Steph nodded, as if she had already known the shape of what was coming, even if not the form.

"And?"

"And? Give me a break. I told him no. I told him I'm not Dad. President… no way." Sarah stood to pour herself a cup of tea.

"You're not dad." Steph said. "But you are his daughter. Never say never."

That night, Sarah lay in bed staring at the ceiling.

"I don't want this," she whispered. "God… find someone else. Please. I'll do your will, but please."

Then she thought of her father. "Oh daddy…If only you were here."

God, come to me. I'm listening."

Silence.

Then a faint voice.

"Sarah."

A little louder.

"Sarah."

A little louder still.

"Sarah."

She sat up.

The voice felt familiar. Internal, but separate. God knocking on her door?

"I'm listening," she said softly.

"You will lead," the voice said. "But not yet."

Her breath steadied.

"Then what is my role?"

"To become."

She closed her eyes.

"If this is You, God, I'm willing. If it's not… then go, depart from me."

Sleep came slowly. And with it, a memory.

Her father, sitting beside her hospital bed.

He had said, "Honey, you won't believe what I saw in Mexico. There's a church where Juan Diego presented a cloak with the image of Mary proving to the Bishop that her message was true. You don't need to demand proof when you pray. Just ask for discernment. God will bring it."

"Proof huh?" she said aloud "Discernment. Hmmm."

She woke before sunrise. Knelt beside her bed. And prayed.

"God our Father, You have a plan for me. You hold out to me a future full of hope. Give me the wisdom of your Spirit so that I can see the shape of your plan in the gifts you have given me, and in the circumstances of my life. Give me the freedom of your Spirit, to seek you with all my heart, and to choose your will above all else. I make this prayer through Christ our Lord. Amen."

Later that morning, a package arrived.

A child from Europe sent it. Nine years old. A note. A drawing of a butterfly.

"Dear Sarah," it read. "I saw you on the news today crying. I'm sorry you lost your father. You may not have your wings yet... but they are coming. When they do, I will follow you. Remember me."

She stared at it.

Then reached into her desk drawer, withdrawing the metal butterfly.

She thought of the man at her father's funeral — the one who had stepped out of the crowd, pressed the metal butterfly into her hand, and said, "Jesus told me you will be President one day. Remember us." Then he had vanished back into the crowd before she could ask his name.

She held it in her hand.

Not yet.

But coming.

And for the first time since her father's passing the heaviness on her heart shifted.

It wasn't gone, but integrating. Grief transmuting to strength with love.

She didn't know what would happen next.

But she did know it would happen as God designs. No pushing. No force needed.

CHAPTER 15
PRESS CONFERENCE

"And they were all filled with the Holy Ghost,
and began to speak with other tongues."
— Acts 2:4

THE ROOM WAS ALREADY full when President Tchi entered.

Lights. Cameras. The noise of reporters anxious for a story.

He moved slower than usual. Still recovering and carrying the heaviness of John's passing—a blow the press wouldn't see coming.

President Zhiyu stood beside him. Composed. Unreadable.

They took their places behind the podium. The room quieted.

Tchi looked out. For a moment, he didn't speak. He had the words, but none of them felt sufficient.

He waited for an inner prompt. "I leave this to you, God." He prayed before speaking.

"Today," he began, "we honor the life of President John Smith."

Cameras stopped flashing. Tchi paused. A collective gasp took the room.

"He changed more than policy. He changed people. And in his passing, he's changing the world."

He spoke of the meeting. Of restraint. Of a path forward. Of a relationship between nations that would no longer be built on fear, but on a freedom and choice neither yet fully understood.

Behind him, screens displayed flags at half-staff.

And then something shifted. At first, it was subtle. A hesitation in the translators' voices. Then they stopped. One by one.

The room stirred. Producers glanced at each other. Technicians checked their feeds.

Tchi continued speaking, unaware anything strange happened.

A reporter in the back — French — lowered her headset. She was hearing him in French. His lips were forming English words.

A man from Brazil looked around, confused. Portuguese. He was hearing Tchi in Portuguese.

Across the world viewers noticed the same thing. No translation. And yet—

everyone heard in their own tongue while Tchi only spoke in English.

The room quietly murmured at first. But it built.

Tchi paused. He felt it. He knew it. A power. Love. Presence. He turned slightly and saw… Him.

Jesus was there.

Seated.

Still.

Watching.

No one moved.

For a moment the air was still, like an ocean tide pulling back before a wave.

A correspondent near the front would tell her husband that night that she felt a warmth, like someone she loved embracing her completely.

A cameraman would say, for the first time since the war, his mind was clear—his hands stopped shaking.

The light in the room seemed brighter, like sun after a cloud clears away.

Then a phone screen brightened.

And another.

The room returned to normal, and the noise began.

Tchi kept calm, but smiled, grateful to experience the mystery others shared from China.

He looked at Zhiyu, who saw Jesus too. Zhiyu smiled and winked.

Reality had shifted.

The cameras kept rolling. Some captured it. Some didn't. Most saw an empty chair. Others—something more.

"Do you see that?" someone whispered.

"Is that—?"

"No… it's a glitch—"

Phones lit up.

Producers shouted.

Clips flooded social media.

Within minutes—the world analyzed a miracle.

"He's there."

"No—there's nothing there."

"Zoom in—zoom in—"

Tchi finished his remarks and stepped back. The room erupted.

Questions. Shouting. Movement.

Zhiyu remained still. Control had always been his strength. But this was not something to control. It was something to face and embrace.

Across the world, the footage spread. Replayed. Debated.

Some were convinced it was Jesus.

Some said it was AI. Phony.

Some claimed it was the beginning, and others the end.

The reigning headline read, "Is this the Second Coming?"

And instantly, with all of it, change happened. Not in governments or institutions, but in people. They transformed in the blink of an eye. They didn't understand it, but felt different. An awakening like no other.

Not everyone embraced it. Some claimed John was the Antichrist—that Jesus had defeated him. Others claimed President Zhiyu was the Antichrist, falsely supporting peace while ushering in a beast system.

People hungered for answers. John's passing had set the perfect *trap* for humanity to find its way.

CHAPTER 16
THREE NIGHTS

"Behold, I stand at the door, and knock: if any man hear my voice, and open the door, I will come in."
— Revelation 3:20

It didn't take long. Confusion mounted. By evening, things had turned.

Crowds gathered in cities across the world. Arguing. Protesting.

Glass shattered. Fires started.

Looting followed.

"You're a fool."

"The end is near."

"Jesus has returned!"

Hidden fears bubbled over searching for something, or someone, to land on.

Those fears needed somewhere to land.

They found targets—Christians among them.

"They've been saying this for years!"

"End times—second coming—a rapture—this is them!"

"They started this!"

It didn't matter that most Christians were just as confused. Unfortunately, fear doesn't wait for clarity, especially when memories are still fresh from war.

In several cities, church doors were shattered. Graffiti warnings appeared on buildings and sidewalks—even as worshipers gathered inside.

A man was dragged from his car after admitting he believed what he saw. Mob rule was real.

Phones recorded everything.

Uploaded instantly.

Shared without context.

Meanwhile, groups of Christians and non-Christians alike gathered in churches to discuss and understand Jesus' appearance.

"What about the rapture? Why are we still here?" One called out.

The pastor tried to explain. "The rapture is not the removal of a person from the world…but the removal of the world from the person. It's when our soul is lifted into Christ…to union with God (*1 Thess. 4:17).*"

"That's not the way I was taught it," someone responded.

"Me either," the pastor responded. "Me either." His face said it all. He was seeking too.

Across the world, the same patterns unfolded. Different languages. Same fears.

Not everyone joined in protest or church. Most hunkered down at home. Praying. Talking. Connecting online. Pulling out their Bibles. A budding revival was brewing alongside the chaos in the streets.

But then another miracle calmed the noise.

As people slept, they entered a dream. Jesus appeared to everyone. Some saw a light, others a man, and still others just heard a voice.

The dreams repeated for three nights. In them, Jesus reclaimed his authority as the son of God.

On the third night, He spoke clearly:

"Watch for a miracle three days from now."

His hands outstretched.

"I am here to return you to the Father…and to reveal what has always been. What I offer is what was always yours."

He paused.

"You will see where you need forgiveness… and where you resist."

"Truth will meet what is false… and what is false will fall away."

"Be alert. The world is being made new… restored."

"Heaven will be realized here."

Invitingly, he said, "Come with me."

"Live like me—whole… united… alive in the Father."

"This is the end… and the beginning."

"Choose me. Or, you can continue resisting."

"It is your choice."

"But all are invited."

"You are invited."

Some woke before the dreams ended.

Some wept as their eyes opened in the new days.

Some forgot within minutes. Some couldn't forget at all.

All were given the dream.

On the morning after the third dream, the world was quiet.

No more riots. No hustling. A peace and a presence was felt.

Questions remained.

"What will the miracle be?" They wondered.

"Should I go to work?"

"Lord, what do you want of me?"

"In my dream He said, 'In three days you will be shown what has always been available to you,'" Sarah said to her siblings.

They gathered over a video conference.

"Me too," Carl said. "And for forty days… our bodies will be restored."

"I know, right?" Elizabeth chimed in. "Sounds impossible to me. I mean… come on… all the sick in the world will be healed for forty days? Why forty days anyway?"

"I think the more important point," Sarah added while scrambling some eggs, "is that those who turn to God during those forty days will be given the antidote for their illness. Those who don't... won't receive what's being offered."

"Seems kind of cruel to me," Elizabeth said. "People have to return to their illnesses if they don't turn back to God? Quite the ultimatum."

"Or not an ultimatum at all," Carl said. "Try it the other way. The forty days isn't a test. It's a gift."

Elizabeth tilted her head. "How do you figure?"

"He's showing us the contrast first — what wholeness actually feels like in the body — and then giving us the answers for how to get there. We're being shown that health was never withheld. It comes from being whole. United with God. Not divided. Not judging. Not running the false-self stories on a loop."

Sarah lifted her coffee mug to the camera. "I agree. When a person is whole, God inspires right action. The right food. The right rest. The right forgiveness. The right work. Right action is what leads to the body's health. Always has." She pauses pondering.

"And it's not always mystical," Sarah added. "Sometimes it's just the doctor's appointment we've been avoiding, or the medication we need to start taking again. The forty days aren't a verdict on us or medicine — they're a reset on what we've forgotten."

"So the forty days..." Elizabeth said slowly.

"Is a preview," Sarah said. "A glimpse of what was always possible. He's encouraging us back to the path that would have gotten us there anyway. Most of the world had rejected it."

"And the ones who don't turn back?" Elizabeth asked.

"Aren't being punished," Sarah said. "They're returning to the same disconnection that made them sick. It's a choice. The healing isn't held back. It's just on the other side of choosing."

Elizabeth was quiet for a moment. "That lands different than how I was hearing it."

"He could heal everyone in an instant and keep us in perfect health forever," Sarah added. "But to what end, if we don't return to God? The healing without the return is just postponement. Now that would be cruel."

"So the point isn't the physical healing?" Elizabeth asked before answering her own question. "It's the restoration."

"Always has been. Dad has been saying that for years." Sarah said.

They fell silent, remembering their father.

"Well, if I choose God. Thank you, Jesus!" Carl exclaimed.

"Me too." Elizabeth echoed.

"Me too." Sarah finished.

Everyone had a choice to make. Each would have to choose.

To be restored in Christ... or to continue resisting God's revelation.

The world had been given something it could not ignore—and something it would not be forced to accept.

CHAPTER 17
SURRENDER

"Father, if thou be willing, remove this cup from me: nevertheless not my will, but thine, be done."
— Luke 22:42

THREE DAYS FOLLOWING the third dream, a man with schizophrenia emerged from his bedroom, clear—present—himself again. His mother, burdened by constant care and worry, looked him over.

"Is that you… really you?"

It was her son, unmasked from the illness.

Across the country, Sarah stood in her kitchen, hands resting on the counter, watching her own reflection in the dark glass of the window.

She felt it before she understood it. Something had lifted. Not just in her body—but everywhere.

At a nearby hospital, a man sat up in bed—moving for the first time in months. The machines whirred and hummed as a startled nurse rushed out of the room, joyfully calling for a doctor.

Down the hall, a song emerged from the lungs of a woman who'd been on a ventilator the night before.

Across the world, children woke with no pain; laughter replaced tears.

The blind could see. The lame walked.

Within hours, something impossible became undeniable.

Sarah's phone wouldn't stop vibrating. Messages stacked faster than she could open them. Videos. Faces. Tears. She answered one call—then another.

"Mom can walk."

"He's talking again."

"They took her off the ventilator."

She covered her mouth, tears forming—not from shock, but recognition.

This is what He said.

People filled the streets, shouting, "Glory be to God. Praise Jesus!"

Hospitals emptied.

Pharmacists filled fewer prescriptions, and the conversations at the counter became more meaningful.

"It's happening."

Three days after the third dream—the world woke up healed.

People fell to their knees, laughed, and prayed. Wept in thanksgiving for God's love pouring through them.

But not everyone celebrated.

"It's temporary," one man said, pacing his living room. "Mass hysteria. It'll pass. Fools."

But it didn't pass.

Churches filled.

Temples overflowed.

The hunger was there. Thanks, praise, and desire to know God more than ever.

People wanted sustained health, sure. But, if God could do this, what else was possible?

Darkness had lifted. Certainty from the past no longer dictated the future.

They didn't understand, but didn't need to. They sought answers—not about why, but how—how to keep their health.

Sarah sat in the back of a small church that afternoon.

The room held anticipation. People leaned forward in their seats. Some held hands. Several stood in the back.

The pastor stood near the altar, fielding questions.

A man called out, "How do I keep this?" he asked, his voice catching slightly. "I don't want to go back."

A woman beside him nodded, hugging her granddaughter, whose hands shook uncontrollably just the day before.

The pastor took his time. Paused longer than expected to answer. He asked the Lord to guide his answers.

"We've prayed for healing before," he said slowly. "But this..." He looked out at them. "This is different. We all know that. It's special. Unprecedented."

Heads nodded. Murmurs of

"Thank you, Jesus." and "Amen." emerged from the congregation.

Sarah lowered her gaze. She wasn't there to listen to the Pastor, but to listen deeper to God's voice in her.

How do we keep this? she wondered.

For a moment, she recognized an old reflex—to understand, so she could know... and then share it to help others.

She breathed. Felt the excitement of becoming the hero, and said under her breath, "I cancel my need to know... to be the hero in this.

I release the urge to create a story that saves people from pain.

I allow them to choose—as I am choosing.

I choose You, God."

The tension melted in her. She settled in her heart. She was there now.

"Now, continue," she heard in her spirit.

"This is the way."

She exhaled, slow and steady.

Stay with Him.

It was confirmation, grounded in love. It was instruction—spiritual formation.

It was her return.

When she lifted her eyes again, the room still buzzed. Nothing had changed. Yet... everything had.

Spiritual leaders of all types leaned on God for guidance as they were called to service at deeper levels.

"How do I stay healthy?"

The answers were no longer theoretical or about someday. They were immediate.

Surrendering their ways. Listening to Jesus. Applying His teachings:

To breathe.

To feel what they had long avoided.

To allow their minds to be renewed—not by force, but by the Spirit of God at work within them.

Judgments softened. Hidden parts surfaced and were integrated with love.

Forgiveness was practiced.

Truth lived.

Trust grew, and with it, transformation.

The hunger was plentiful as these concepts were present, real, and timely.

Not everyone turned to God. Some resisted quietly. Others loudly.

Social feeds filled with explanations, denials, and alternative theories.

"The elites did this."

"It's a trick."

"Proof of aliens."

"It's temporary."

"It's of the devil."

"This isn't God."

Across the world, the same tension unfolded: wonder and resistance, faith and fear.

In Beijing, Zhiyu sat with his advisors, listening as reports came in—healings, unrest, devotion, denial. He did not respond immediately, but watched.

And somewhere amidst the weight of leadership, something moved within him—humility.

Meanwhile, at the White House, President Tchi stood overlooking the Rose Garden, caught between awe and responsibility.

He thought of John. "Did you have something to do with all this?" he whispered, imagining John's mission continuing with Jesus somehow in Heaven.

"This is really something. Beautiful… but chaotic."

Knowing he had to do something, he acted.

For one day—on every platform—a single message was shared from the White House.

It was a video of Sarah sitting beside a painting of her father; drawing on the fond memory of his legacy.

"You remember the dream," she said. "You are always and ever will be one with God. This health… this incredible health we are all receiving is a precious gift. It will last forty days."

Her eyes held steady.

"And then… things will return."

She paused, knowing the weight her words would carry to listeners.

"Remember also that Jesus gave us a way forward."

She leaned toward the camera and continued.

"If you turn to God—not out of fear, but from the core of your being—you will be shown a path to continue in this health.

"That path will look different for each of us—a prayer, a call to a friend, mourning a loss, visiting a doctor… All of it is God working. Healing comes in many shapes."

Sarah smiled and paused.

"No one has to do this," she said. "It's a choice for all of us.

My father talked about this my whole life. '*Jesus is here. Heaven is closer than my breath. God is in us and with us and everywhere. He only wants us to return Home, and Jesus is showing us the way.*' That was our dinner conversation."

She looked over her shoulder, tears forming, and took a breath.

"Thank you, Dad."

Looking back with conviction, she said, "Something is happening that may never occur again. We are all the prodigal sons and daughters being called home. I, for one, will be making my peace with my past, practicing what Jesus shared. Returning to Him fully."

"I feel it in my soul. The invitation. My fellow citizens, we are being asked to live in Christ and walk with our Father in Heaven now. Let go of what you made God to be and invite God in as God is. Bless you."

The message ended.

Sarah sat there for a moment after the recording stopped. No one spoke, giving her space. Confidence settled within her. She was on the right path, in flow with her mission.

As her message spread, something in the world shifted again.

The commotion calmed.

Church had left the buildings—permeating every breath.

For forty days, the world lived differently.

People forgave.

Called those they hadn't spoken to in years.

Sat in silence.

Prayed without scripts.

Space was made whole. People acted from love.

Sarah found herself doing the same.

Calling old friends from Kentucky. Walking alone by the river. Letting things surface she once pushed away.

Her return went deeper.

Just as quickly as the world became accustomed to the new reality, it stopped.

The forty days ended.

Illnesses returned. They didn't rush back, but seeped in like something familiar finding its way back.

Sarah felt it the moment it began. She questioned, *Did I do enough? Am I ready?*

Those who had returned to God soon received insights, like divine downloads and prompts that directed them to solutions.

In Detroit, a man received two sentences: *Call Dr. Jonus. Tell him about the pain and the rash.* He called. He went. The diagnosis was treatable. The healing came through a surgeon's hands — and through the courage to say aloud what he'd been hiding. Both were of God.

Some trusted the prompts right away, and others resisted.

"Go to the cemetery and dance? I'm not doing that," one elderly woman said to her family.

"But don't you remember how much you and Dad loved to dance?" Her daughter encouraged.

As the days passed and pains returned to the old woman's body, her resistance fell, and she said, "Fine… I'll go do a jig, I guess."

Her daughter drove her—witnessed a miracle. There she was, at 93 years old, dancing, as best she could, near her husband's grave.

Soon, memories flooded her mind. "I'll never dance again, Norman, until Jesus himself dances with me," were the last words she spoke to her husband before he passed.

She stopped and laughed. "Funny. Very funny, Jesus. You got me. I get it. I love you." She didn't hear a response, but the pain… It left, almost instantly.

Stories of divine guidance ranged from super-ordinary to super-natural. Sometimes health returned in one prompt, and others took hundreds. They all led to restoration, healing—spiritual wholeness first… emotional… mental… and often physical.

The key: Trust. Trusting the prompt was for them. That their path was theirs—not copying or comparing, but designed for them.

Some failed—returning to old patterns. Still searching. Still resisting. Still asking.

But no one was abandoned. Everyone could choose. Sarah knew it. Zhiyu felt it.

And the world, for the first time, understood the weight of that choice.

CHAPTER 18
REVELATION

"Christ has no body now but yours.
No hands, no feet on earth but yours. Yours are the eyes through which he looks compassion on this world."
— St. Teresa of Ávila

THE NEXT SEVERAL years unfolded like a rebirth of civilization.

Rhythms quickened. Innovations followed. Collaborations expanded. Peace held. The changes were undeniable. The mysteries incredible.

Some claimed to see Jesus return on the clouds. No recordings ever confirmed it. Still, enough people had seen… enough people had experienced… that proof was no longer necessary for believers.

The New Jerusalem, referenced in Revelation, was no longer anticipated. It was being lived.

It spread through people, choices, and surrender. It took root in the way people lived—especially among the young, who began to transform naturally. On time. No agendas.

As caterpillars naturally transform to butterflies, people naturally transformed to living in Christ. The masks were gone, or didn't last long. Resistance became nearly impossible as so much love embodied the planet.

In a small town in Kentucky, people gathered at Old Hickory church.

They came from all over. Some were invited. Others felt called in the spirit to attend.

Some had walked closely with John. Others had only heard the stories.

Sarah stood near the edge of a nearby field, taking it in. Tents, BBQs, and praying inside and outside.

Colette approached her, walking with strength—her cane gone. For a moment, neither spoke. Then they embraced, remembering the sacred beginning of their relationship. Two parts of the same story, meeting again.

"He would love this," Colette said softly.

Sarah smiled, her eyes filling. "Yes. But, small correction. He does love this."

They stepped back, looking out over the gathering.

Children ran freely, playing tag amongst the adults.

A circle of mothers prayed over a mother-to-be.

Colette hesitated for a moment, then smiled—almost like she had been waiting for the right time.

"I brought something," Colette said.

"Oh? Do tell." Sarah anticipated another of Colette's notebooks filled with Jesus stories, adventures to enliven the Gospel even more.

Colette laughed softly, then reached inside a worn leather bag. She carefully lifted a linen-wrapped bundle.

She held it with both hands, honoring what was inside.

"I wasn't sure if this was the right place," she said. "But now… I know it is."

Sarah's expression softened as Colette gently unfolded the linen. A small glass box emerged, outlined by a simple metal frame.

Inside, Sarah saw the bundle of strands, resting quietly, as they had for centuries.

"Oh my…" she said.

"I was entrusted with this," Colette said. "It's been hidden… protected. Moved across time. Always with the same belief… that it mattered."

She paused.

"It did matter," Sarah said gently.

Colette traced the relic's history — from now back through 1930, all the way to 1517. Sarah listened, taking it in—the story stretching back through time, now resting in her.

Colette nodded. "I was asked to bring it to Washington. But seeing you… coming here… maybe I'll take it to Mexico City… somewhere people could see and honor it—an early reminder of His presence with us."

She looked up at the church. At the people. At Christ alive in all of it. Then back down at Sarah.

"But now…" she said quietly, "…I'm not so sure."

Sarah stepped closer and put her arm around Colette.

"That relic carried something through time. Through people who believed. Now… He's revealed Himself again."

Colette looked at her, searching.

"And?"

Sarah looked to the sky.

"Now it points."

She placed her hand gently over her own heart. "Not in a box," she said. "…but here."

Colette exhaled. The weight of the relic's responsibility fell from her.

They stood together in silence. The box still visible between them. Still honored, but no longer needed in the same way.

A hymn started at the church and made its way through the crowd. Sarah and Colette moved toward the church to join the others.

The Spirit of God was moving.

Colette carefully wrapped the box again and winked at Sarah.

"Maybe it still has a place," she said.

Sarah nodded. "It does."

Across the field, Sarah caught sight of Steph near one of the tents. Tchi stood beside her, sleeves rolled up, a paper plate in one hand. A small detail of agents stood at a respectful distance — earpieces in, eyes scanning, but giving them space. Tchi had come quietly, with as small a footprint as the office allowed. No press. Just a friend, here for a friend.

He said something Sarah couldn't hear, and Steph laughed — really laughed, the way she used to before any of this.

Sarah smiled.

Two people who had each held more than most could bear found a moment of lightness back at Old Hickory, where John's legacy began. Their losses would not be forgotten. Their laughter would carry far and wide.

Steph caught Sarah's eye and waved. Sarah lifted her hand in return.

That's a gift, she thought.

Later, as the sun began to lower, someone spoke John's name. It wasn't brought up that he was president, pastor, or machinist. But a man… who said yes.

Stories followed. Moments. Memories. The quiet ways he listened. The bold ways he obeyed.

Sarah listened more than she spoke.

At one point a young man — not yet thirty, hands rough from work — caught her eye across the field and made his way over.

"How do I become like him?" he asked.

Sarah thought a moment and responded, "You don't. You become the one who says *yes* where you are… in your life and for your mission. Dad never asked for or wanted people following him. He wanted to honor God, and in that helped his *neighbors* know God."

The young man said, "Thank you. I like that. I can do that."

As evening settled in, a stillness came over the space. A presence.

The same presence that had come in the dreams… that had healed, and called them Home.

It was there.

Within.

Among.

Sarah closed her eyes and smiled knowingly. Centered, she exhaled.

Stay with Him. Perhaps there is no need to wait for another coming… if we stay with Him.

The world will continue. There is more to learn. More to release. More to nurture. More to love.

The New Jerusalem will expand… through those willing to live it. Maybe not perfectly. But honestly… authentically.

Praise God!

And bless you. May you find your way with God—into restoration, transformation, and full expression.

May the Next Second Coming… return through you.

EPILOGUE

For those saying yes to the Next Second Coming returning through you — a prayer, and an invitation

Prayer With Me:

Take a breath. Speak it slowly. There's no wrong way.

Heavenly Father,

I know not how, but I remember You — Your love, and the life You give.

I am thankful for everything. And though I have said things I regret and done things against You, I seek forgiveness. I release my judgments — of myself, of others, of Your world.

Make me new. Change me. Bring forth Your life force and cleanse me. Purify me. I'm willing.

Send Your Holy Spirit to guide and train my soul, my mind, my body. Prepare me to live in Christ.

And I say yes to Jesus. I fear not, for You are with me.

Amen.

Beyond the Book:

Join us at theocoalition for books, the practical application of Jesus' teachings, and camaraderie along the way.

ACKNOWLEDGMENTS

There is a lifetime of love from many who have been in my life for a moment, a season, or the whole *ride*.

This book has a few standout contributors who helped bring it into focus, make it better, and deliver value.

PROFESSIONAL TEAM:

You worked tirelessly to help create a story that is readable, enjoyable, and useful:

To Thought Leader Press / Signature Message, including the amazing **Leanne Huffman**, **Stefan Junaeus,** and team. Strategy, developmental edit, final edit, layout, publishing, and more. Thank you for continuing to make this powerful series a success.

To **Milabookcovers.com** for the cover design. You listened to the concept, took input well, revised graciously, and nailed the cover! Great work.

To **Minista Jazz**, founder of muchdifferentworld.com and creator of my Digital Double. Jazz is a former global hairstylist turned self-taught technologist and founder of a digital identity trust to ensure that I (and others) own, protect, and consent to the use of our voice, image, and likeness in the age of AI.

Useful Technology:

I so appreciate technology!

***Images*:** Adobe and ChatGPT helped me find or co-create images for the chapters

Edits: ChatGPT and Claude helped me in four ways:

1. Cross-reference Bible passages with history to anchor fiction with actuality.
2. Identify errors in grammar and punctuation fast.
3. Identify and close inconsistencies and loops in the story.
4. Brainstorm ideas following the developmental edit review.

Research: Biblegateway.com, *ChatGPT, and more*

MENTORS AND EARLY READERS:

Pre-release readers are critical to get a story from good to great. The *bones* of this story were strong, but the beauty of it only came following real people reading and responding. Thank you —with all my heart:

Alison Ooms, Amy Lau, Angie Bruce, Brad Lively, Dawn Kristy, Eric Himes, Gene Huneycutt, Gina Johnson, James Chitwood, Jim McGough, Joseph Gabriel, Keith A. Little, Melissa G. Wilson, Michael Ryce, Paige Junaeus, Rex Montague Bauer

FAMILY

Prayers, love, and support go a long way. I run ideas past friends and family. Many hours of effort. Inconveniences from time to time. Incoherent concepts at times. Process. Maturing. Reconciliation. Excitement and frustration. Refining. The pages of my life mirrored in stories. All this requires love, patience, and consideration. Thank you to Liz and Sophie for listening when you don't necessarily want to. It helps. Thank you, Liz, for trusting the process even when it is not logical.

WHAT'S NEXT?

1. *HEAR FROM MARK – VIDEO*

2. *USE DISCUSSION GUIDE IN NEXT SECTION OF THIS BOOK*

Whether alone, with a friend, in a book club, or at a church small group, these questions are for you. See *Church Small Group* below for more free support resources.

---

3. ***BEYOND** THE NEXT SECOND COMING*

John's church is a real vision. We meet at The O Coalition to put these teachings to work in everyday life — together. Join us. You'll find camaraderie, more stories, and a deeper understanding of who you are, what you're for, and how the divisions keeping you from God can finally fall. (And ask me about my Digital Double when you arrive.) **theocoalition.com**

4. *CHURCH SMALL GROUP*

Run a Small Group study around this book. The Discussion Guide in your hands maps to eight sessions. Free leader materials — session plans, facilitator notes, scripture cross-references — are at **theocoalition.com/tnsc-smallgroup**.

5. *SHARE*

- **Gift your copy** (or a new one) to a friend, colleague, or loved one.
- **Post** a photo of you with your book. Add a few words of how it moved you, challenged you, inspired you.

6. *WRITE A REVIEW*

Your review is how this book finds the next reader. If something in these pages mattered to you, please leave a review on Amazon: **theocoalition.com/tnsc-review**

7. *INVITE MARK TO SPEAK*

Mark speaks at churches, retreats, conferences, book clubs, and leadership gatherings on the themes at the heart of this book series — saying yes to God in ordinary life, the inner work of the next second coming, the Beatitudes, and the practical application of Jesus's teachings for everyday leaders. Inquire about availability at **theocoalition.com/tnsc-speak**.

READER COMPANION MATERIALS

For

THE NEXT SECOND COMING

Book Four of The O Coalition

Mark Hattas

These materials are offered as companions, not commentaries. They invite discussion, deeper understanding, and application. Use them in book clubs, prayer groups, or alone with a cup of coffee and a Bible at the elbow.

DISCUSSION GUIDE

Eight sessions — thirty-two questions — designed for book clubs, small groups, and contemplative reading. Each section gathers two or three chapters and opens with an orienting paragraph before the questions begin.

How to use this guide

Read the assigned chapters before you gather. Open the session with the section's opening paragraph read aloud. Move through the questions at whatever pace honors the room — four good questions slowly are better than thirty rushed. Close with silence, prayer, or the chapter's epigraph (see verses below chapter headings).

SECTION 1 — THE CALLING

Chapters 1–3 · God, Are You There?, The Relic, Old Hickory

The book opens with John in church, asking the same question he has asked since he was a teenager: God, are you there? The answer comes through stillness, through two visions stretching back centuries — Jericho preparing Jerusalem for Jesus's arrival in 1517, and a hidden relic discovered in 1932 that proves the visit was real. Then the lens widens to John's own history: the angle grinder that almost killed him, his first wife's death, the message in the sky at her funeral — "Build my church" — and the slow obedience that made Old Hickory what it is. By the time Colette walks through the door, John has already been preparing for years without knowing it.

1. 1"I'll go. I'll go." — John yells those words after the angle grinder almost takes his face. Has there been a moment in your life when fear or near-loss became the doorway to a yes? What did you say afterward, and to whom?
2. The 1517 vision shows a Jesus who has visited before — a return already lived in the Damascus Gate Plaza. What stayed with Jericho, more than Christ's words, was what happened to the people listening: "Everything twisted in them seemed to come undone." What in you most needs to come undone right now?
3. The drone show at Janie's funeral spells out "Build my church" — a message no one programmed. Where in your life has guidance arrived through an instrument that was unexplainable? What did you do with it?
4. John's church begins as a complement to Sunday — multifaith, intimate, focused on practical application of Jesus's teachings rather than competition with the existing church. If you started your own gathering of a half-dozen people tomorrow, what would it be for, and who would you invite first?

SECTION 2 — COLETTE'S WITNESS

Chapters 4–5 · Colette, Prophetic Mystery

Colette tells her own story. Childhood visions of cherubim and seraphim filling her church's sanctuary — wheels within wheels, four faces each. Jesus stepping out of the Eucharist at age five and holding her hand. A notebook from fourteen, full of teachings received in the empty thirty minutes after morning mass — and the language of angels flowing through her before she had a name for tongues. Then the harder turn: the second coming she was shown is layered — what already happened in 70 A.D. with the destruction of Jerusalem and the Temple, and what is still happening inside the reader. By the time she leaves the room, she has named the Antichrist as something living within.

5. Colette's mysticism is concrete — the angels, the Eucharist, a hand held at age five, the language of angels at fourteen. How does the book treat mystical experience as evidence rather than imagination? Where does that land for you, and where does it ask you to stretch?
6. The historical fulfillment of Matthew 24 in 70 A.D. — Theudas, Caligula, the destruction of Jerusalem and the Temple — is presented as a real first layer of Christ's return. What did this reading of prophecy do to your sense of the end times?
7. Colette teaches that scripture works in layers — plain meaning, hint, deeper interpretation, and mystery — and that the deeper layer of the second coming is "Christ emerging in union with you." Have you ever read scripture and discovered a layer you hadn't seen before? What changed?
8. "The Antichrist lives in us — in every part where we block transformation in Christ." Where in your life is

something blocking that transformation right now? What would it cost to release it? What could be if you embraced it?

SECTION 3 — THE CRUCIBLE

Chapters 6–7 · The Accident, The Basilica

A railroad dream interpreted as the inner track of Christ being laid. A semi-truck swerves and Sarah is in a coma. A vanished stranger gives her mouth-to-mouth. Jesus tells John to leave his comatose daughter and his furious wife and fly to Mexico City — and at the Basilica of Our Lady of Guadalupe, in a sacred garden in front of a centuries-old image, John hears Mary speak: "Am I not here, I who am your mother?" Sarah wakes the next morning. She remembers seeing him there. The marital question Mary asked John to bring home — "Will you love me enough to trust Christ?" — has already been put to Steph at three a.m. The phone rings. Washington is calling.

9. *The dream interpreter tells John he is the engineer of an inner track — a path beneath the waters that once separated humankind from God, transforming those depths into a means of travel. Where in your life is the inner track being laid? What waters are you being asked to pass through? And, when a dream felt like a message from God in your life?*
10. *Steph rushes home from overseas to a comatose daughter, and John leaves anyway. The book treats this as obedience rather than abandonment — and Steph's text "Go" makes the obedience possible. Have you ever had to choose between two genuinely competing goods? How did you discern which yes was the right one?*

11. *Mary appears in the sacred garden in Mexico City and her words to John echo what she said to Juan Diego in 1531: "Am I not here, I who am your mother?" How does the book treat Marian devotion — and what does Mary's role in this chapter open or challenge for you?*
12. *Steph hears "Will you love me enough to trust Christ?" at three a.m., before John ever asks her. Two people receive the same word. Has the Spirit ever spoken the same thing to you and someone close to you, separately and at the same time? What did that confirmation make possible?*

SECTION 4 — GOING PUBLIC

Chapters 8–10 · DC, Jesus Take the Wheel, See The Forest!

John arrives at the White House and is asked to lead a spiritual council that has no precedent — five members of the President's staff have seen his face shown to them by Jesus. The Italian from Mexico City turns out to be the Secretary of Defense. Three months later, in a dinner that quietly redefines what political wisdom looks like, John leads President Tchi through a practice of canceling control, releasing judgment, and listening for Christ's voice. The Holy Spirit confirms a Russian deception none of the intelligence had caught. A vision of Putin underwater reveals a global alliance built without the United States. And John tells the President a teaching that reinforces the spine of the book: "Heaven makes a home in the purified soul, and the world loses its power over that person."

13. *The five who saw John's face had a code: "Jesus is coming at this very moment." Colette's visit to Old Hickory was the test. How does the book treat divine confirmation — through faces, codes, witnesses, dreams — and what would*

change about your discernment if you started taking such confirmations seriously?

14. *President Tchi's first instinct is to delegate the spiritual work to John. John refuses: "You can't have me breathe for you, walk for you, speak for you, or do this for you, sir. Only you can align your soul." Where in your life have you tried to outsource the work that only you can do?*
15. *The "ocean as a shield" hides a forest beneath. What illusions in your own life have you mistaken for reality? What would seeing through them require?*
16. *John reframes the Last Judgment: "Every end is just a new beginning. The path is not to achieve an end. It is to live eternally as one in being with our Creator." How does this reframing change — or not change — how you read Revelation, eschatology, and your own death?*

SECTION 5 — THE WORLD STAGE

Chapters 11–13 · The Summit, China, Healing Worlds

The summit gathers leaders from one hundred fifty-six nations and the Vice President takes a bullet meant for the President. A Chinese ruler hears his mother's favorite story told by a Kentucky machinist and asks for a private word. By June, John is Vice President. By October, after Tchi's body fails, he is President. The night before flying to China — into the dragon's mouth, by his own admission — Jesus visits and walks him through the Book of Revelation as inner architecture: the throne already seated within, the Lamb joining awareness, the seals breaking pride and fear and apathy, the beast as ego, Babylon as everything we built to achieve God. Then in Beijing, across from President Zhiyu, John names what cannot be forced. Jesus appears in the room. John takes his hand and goes home.

17. *The Vice President steps across the President's path without knowing why and takes the bullet. The book calls it "a terrible mercy." How do you sit with stories where God's protection looks like someone else's death?*
18. *Jesus walks John through Revelation as inner journey rather than external prophecy — the throne within every heart, the seals as hidden layers of the self, Babylon as the false self collapsing. Does this reading deepen Revelation for you, or thin it? Where do you land between the literal and the symbolic?*
19. *The Mark of the Beast, John says, "isn't placed on a person… it's agreed to. When a person decides — consciously or not — that they must secure their life apart from God." Where in your life is fear of survival masquerading as wisdom? What would unmasking it cost?*
20. *John dies mid-sentence in Beijing, taking Jesus's hand because his "race was over." How does the book's treatment of his death — gentle, mid-mission, without warning — change your perception of obedience and its costs?*

SECTION 6 — THE CHARGE

Chapters 14–15 · Right Action, Press Conference

The charge passes from John to Sarah. Zhiyu flies to Washington unsettled. Tchi answers his question — Control or Invite? — with one word. Zhiyu decides to try John's way. He offers Sarah the presidency; she declines. Then God speaks to her in the dark: "You will lead. But not yet." Her role is "To become." A nine-year-old child sends a drawing of a butterfly: "Your wings are coming." At the press conference, Tchi speaks English and the world hears him in their own languages — Pentecost in reverse. Jesus is seated, watching. People transform in the blink of an eye. The headline runs: "Is this the Second Coming?" And the world begins to find out.

21. *"You will lead. But not yet." How does the book treat formation as the work that precedes office? Where in your life are you in the becoming, not yet in the leading?*
22. *The reverse Pentecost — one English voice heard in every language — undoes the confusion of Babel. What does the book seem to suggest about the end of separation, and where do you see that already happening in your life, community or family?*
23. *Sarah remembers her father's teaching about Juan Diego: "Don't demand proof when you pray. Just ask for discernment." Where in your life are you asking for proof when discernment is what's available?*
24. *The Antichrist accusation runs in both directions — some say John was, some say Zhiyu is. The book treats this kind of mirror-accusation as part of the pattern. How do you discern between prophetic warning and projection — in others, and in yourself?*

SECTION 7 — THE CHOICE

Chapters 16–17 · Three Nights, Surrender

The world's first reaction is fear. Riots and looting. Christians scapegoated. A pastor reframes the rapture: not the removal of a person from the world, but the removal of the world from the person. Then for three nights Jesus appears in everyone's dreams: "Choose me. Or, you can continue resisting. But all are invited." Three days later, the world wakes healed — schizophrenia lifted, ventilators silent, the lame walking. For forty days. Sarah, in a small church, surrenders the hero reflex: "I cancel my need to know… to be the hero in this." Then the forty days end. Illnesses seep back. But for those who stayed with the practice, prompts begin — go to the cemetery and dance. Some failed. None were abandoned.

25. *The rapture as "the removal of the world from the person, not the person from the world." How does that reframe land for you? Where does it open a door, and where does it ask too much?*
26. *Carl reframes the forty days: "It's not an ultimatum. It's a gift. He's showing us the contrast first — what wholeness actually feels like — and then giving us the answers for how to get there." Has there been a "forty days" in your life — a season of unusual grace that you understood only afterward as preview, not permanence?*
27. *Sarah cancels the need to be the hero. "I release the urge to create a story that saves people from pain. I allow them to choose — as I am choosing." Where in your life are you trying to save someone from the choice that is theirs to make?*
28. *The ninety-three-year-old woman dances at her husband's gravestone because God's prompt told her to, and the pain leaves. The prompts in this chapter are personal, idiosyncratic, sometimes silly. What is the smallest, strangest prompt you've received from God? What happened when you followed it — or didn't?*

SECTION 8 — THE NEW LIFE

CHAPTER 18 AND EPILOGUE • REVELATION, PRAY WITH ME

Years later. At Old Hickory. People come from everywhere — some who walked with John, some who only heard the stories. Colette arrives without her cane, carrying a glass box that holds the strands of hair from 1517. Sarah lays a hand over her own heart: "Now it points. Not in a box. Here." Steph and Tchi laugh together over paper plates. Stories of John pass through the field — not the President or the pastor or the machinist, but "a man who said yes." As evening settles, the same presence that came in the dreams arrives again. Sarah closes her eyes and finds the book's final teaching: "Stay with Him. Perhaps there is no need to wait for another coming… if we stay with Him." The Epilogue opens its hands toward the reader. The next coming returns through you.

29. *Sarah's insight — "Stay with Him. There is no need to wait for another coming if we stay with Him" — resolves the entire book. What changes in your life if the second coming has already happened, is happening, and is still coming, all at once?*
30. *Colette brings the relic to Old Hickory and finds it is no longer needed in the same way. Sarah names where it lives now: in the heart. Where in your life are you holding a sacred object — literal or symbolic — that has done its work and is ready to be relocated or released?*
31. *The book closes with John remembered not as president, pastor, or machinist, but as "a man who said yes." If your life were summarized in a single word like that, what would the word be — and what would you want it to be?*
32. *The closing prayer is offered, not required. If you said the prayer aloud — slowly, in your own voice — what is the next thing you would do today? What is the first thing you would stop doing?*

DID THE QUESTIONS RESONATE?

Prayerfully consider leading your first Small Group study around *The Next Second Coming*, or your next one. Beyond the Discussion Guide in your hands, free leader materials such as session plans, facilitator notes, scripture cross-references — are available for you at **theocoalition.com/tnsc-small group**.

GLOSSARY

Terms a reader may meet for the first time in this book — or meet again in unfamiliar dress. Definitions are written for the curious general reader, not for the scholar.

Antichrist. Used in the book in its Johannine sense — not a single end-times figure but the spirit that denies Christ's presence in flesh and in neighbor (1 John 4:3). The book treats it as a posture more than a person.

Basilica. A major Catholic church granted special status by the Pope. The book's Roman scenes unfold inside such a space — chosen for its weight of gathered prayer.

Carillon. A set of tuned bells played from a keyboard, common in cathedrals. Bells in the book function as thresholds — marking the move from ordinary to sacred time.

Cherubim and Seraphim. The two highest orders of angels in Christian and Jewish angelology. Seraphim ("burning ones") appear in Isaiah 6; cherubim guard sacred space (Genesis 3:24). Both surface in the book's mystical imagery.

Communion / Eucharist. The Christian sacrament of bread and wine remembering Christ's last supper. Catholic theology holds that the elements truly become Christ's body and blood (transubstantiation); Protestant traditions vary. The book takes the Catholic frame seriously without insisting on it.

Eightfold Path. The Buddhist framework for ending suffering: right view, intention, speech, action, livelihood, effort, mindfulness, and concentration. The book holds it alongside Christian ethics rather than against.

Fiat. Latin for "let it be done." The word for Mary's yes at the Annunciation (Luke 1:38) and the template for every consenting yes in the book.

Marian Apparition. An appearance of the Virgin Mary to a witness or witnesses. The Church investigates such claims rigorously; only a handful are formally approved. Guadalupe (1531) is among the most consequential and is woven through the book.

New Jerusalem. The renewed city descending from heaven in Revelation 21 — not destruction but consummation. The book's ending leans toward this image rather than the fire-and-brimstone alternative.

Our Lady of Guadalupe. The 1531 apparition of Mary to Juan Diego near Mexico City, leaving an image on his tilma that remains physically unexplained. The book treats Guadalupe as a hinge between indigenous and European spiritual lineages.

PaRDeS. A Hebrew acronym for the four classical layers of scriptural interpretation: Peshat (plain meaning), Remez (hint), Derash (interpretation), and Sod (mystery). The book reads scripture in all four registers.

Pentecost. The descent of the Holy Spirit on the disciples fifty days after Easter (Acts 2). Tongues of fire, many languages understood as one. The book inverts the image — many voices speaking a single truth.

Prodigal Son. The parable in Luke 15 of the son who leaves, fails, and is welcomed home by a father who runs to meet him. The book uses it as a portrait of God's posture toward every reader.

Psalm 91. The protection psalm. "He that dwelleth in the secret place of the most High shall abide under the shadow of the Almighty." Quoted and lived inside the narrative.

Rapture. The end-times catching-up of believers described in 1 Thessalonians 4:17 and elaborated in nineteenth-century Protestant theology. The book references the imagery without endorsing the typical timeline.

Right Action. The ethical limb of the Buddhist Eightfold Path — conduct that does no harm. The book treats it as a near-cousin to the Christian fruits of the Spirit (Galatians 5).

Sermon on the Mount. Christ's teaching in Matthew 5–7 — the Beatitudes, the Lord's Prayer, love of enemies. The ethical and spiritual spine of the book extended from its foundation in Book One: *The Lowly Prophet*.

Speaking in Tongues. Also known as glossolalia. In Acts 2 it functions as understanding across languages; in 1 Corinthians 12–14 as a spiritual gift requiring interpretation. The book uses both senses.

Tao. Chinese for "the way." In Taoist philosophy, the unnameable order of reality. The book occasionally lets it stand beside the Greek logos of John 1.

Tilma. A traditional Mexican peasant's cloak, woven from cactus fiber. The cloak that bears the image of Our Lady of Guadalupe — still extant, still unexplained.

Transubstantiation. The Catholic doctrine that the bread and wine of the Eucharist become — in substance, though not in appearance — the body and blood of Christ. Defined at the Fourth Lateran Council (1215).

Trinity. The Christian doctrine of one God in three persons — Father, Son, Holy Spirit. The book frames marriage and friendship as small icons of this relational unity.

Twinkling of an Eye. Paul's phrase in 1 Corinthians 15:52 for the moment of resurrection — sudden, complete, beyond chronology. Used in the book to describe how a yes can change everything at once.

Vessel. Biblical word for a person who carries the holy without being its source (2 Corinthians 4:7 — "this treasure in earthen vessels"). John, in the book, is a vessel; the protagonist is Christ.

ENDNOTES

1. *Theudus and Judas: Antiquities* 20.97–99 and Acts 5:36–37
2. Eusebius (*Hist. Eccl.* 3.5) records that believers escaped to Pella in the Decapolis before Jerusalem fell.
3. The Veil Breaker (book 2) reference
4. Chapter 4: **Peshat → Remez → Derash → Sod** framework without sounding technical is from Messianic Prophecy Revealed by Rabbi Kirt A Schneider

ABOUT THE AUTHOR

Mark Hattas is a successful entrepreneur and author. He is passionate about introducing people to the powerful practices Jesus shared for happiness and fulfillment.

Mark went through a massive transformation following the sale of his tech business in 2010. Today, God's asked Mark to write and build The O Coalition. He writes fiction novels that deepen faith in people hungry to know God and live their optimal lives.

His attitude about writing: Surrender to God and allow the story to come—how every book in the series has excelled to deliver on its unique promises.

The O Coalition collection began with book one, The Lowly Prophet, which became a #1 best-seller and winner of many awards. Enjoy the whole series and more at theocoalition.com.

www.ingramcontent.com/pod-product-compliance
Lightning Source LLC
LaVergne TN
LVHW090513110826
845146LV00003B/846

* 9 7 9 8 9 9 2 9 3 6 6 7 4 *